Studies in Wi

Marie Belloc Lowndes

Alpha Editions

This edition published in 2024

ISBN : 9789364739825

Design and Setting By
Alpha Editions
www.alphaedis.com
Email - info@alphaedis.co

As per information held with us this book is in Public Domain.

This book is a reproduction of an important historical work. Alpha Editions uses the best technology to reproduce historical work in the same manner it was first published to preserve its original nature. Any marks or number seen are left intentionally to preserve its true form.

Contents

I ....- 1 -
ALTHEA'S OPPORTUNITY ....- 1 -

II ....- 21 -
MR. JARVICE'S WIFE ....- 21 -

III ....- 42 -
A VERY MODERN INSTANCE ....- 42 -

IV ....- 68 -
ACCORDING TO MEREDITH ....- 68 -

V ....- 92 -
SHAMEFUL BEHAVIOUR? ....- 92 -

VI ....- 124 -
THE DECREE MADE ABSOLUTE ....- 124 -

I

ALTHEA'S OPPORTUNITY

"His confidence shall be rooted out of his tabernacle, and it shall bring him to the king of terrors."—JOB xviii. 14.

There came the sound of a discreet, embarrassed cough, and Althea Scrope turned quickly round from the window by which she had been standing still dressed in her outdoor things.

She had heard the door open, the unfolding of the tea-table, the setting down of the tea-tray, but her thoughts had been far away from the old house in Westminster which was now her home; her thoughts had been in Newcastle, dwelling for a moment among the friends of her girlhood, for whom she had been buying Christmas gifts that afternoon.

The footman's cough recalled her to herself, and to the present.

"Am I to say that you are at home this afternoon, ma'am?"

Althea's thoughtful, clear eyes rested full on the youth's anxious face. He had not been long in the Scropes' service, and this was the first time he had been left in such a position of responsibility, but Dockett, the butler, was out, a rare event, for Dockett liked to be master in his master's house. Before the marriage of Perceval Scrope, Dockett had been Scrope's valet, and, as Althea was well aware, the man still regarded her as an interloper. Althea did not like Dockett, but Perceval was very fond of him, and generally spoke of him to his friends as "Trip." Althea had never been able to discover the reason of the nickname, and she had not liked to ask; her husband often spoke a language strange to her.

"I will see Mr. Bustard if he comes," she said gently.

Dockett would not have disturbed her by asking the question, for Dockett always knew, by a sort of instinct, whom his master and mistress wished to see or to avoid seeing.

Again she turned and stared out of the high, narrow, curtainless windows. Perceval Scrope did not like curtains, and so of course there were no curtains in his wife's drawing-room.

Snow powdered the ground. It blew in light eddies about the bare branches of the trees marking the carriage road through St. James's Park, and was caught in whirling drifts on the frozen sheet of water which reflected the lights on the bridge spanning the little lake. Even at this dreary time of the year it was a charming outlook, and one which most of Althea's many acquaintances envied her.

And yet the quietude of the scene at which she was gazing so intently oppressed her, and, suddenly, from having felt warm after her walk across the park, Althea Scrope felt cold.

She moved towards the fireplace, and the flames threw a red glow on her tall, rounded figure, creeping up from the strong serviceable boots to the short brown skirt, and so to the sable cape which had been one of her husband's wedding gifts, but which now looked a little antiquated in cut and style.

It is a bad thing—a sign that all is not right with her—when a beautiful young woman becomes indifferent to how she looks. This was the case with Althea, and yet she was only twenty-two, and looked even younger; no one meeting her by chance would have taken her to be a married woman, still less the wife of a noted politician.

She took off her fur cape and put it on a chair. She might have sent for her maid, but before her marriage she had always waited on herself, and she was not very tidy—one of her few points of resemblance with her husband, and not one which made for harmony. But Mrs. Scrope, if untidy, was also conscientious, and as she looked at the damp fur cloak her conscience began to trouble her.

She rang the bell. "Take my cloak and hang it up carefully in the hall," she said to the footman. And now the room was once more neat and tidy as she knew her friend, Mr. Bustard, would like to see it.

It was a curious and delightful room, but it resembled and reflected the woman who had to spend so much of her life there as little as did her quaint and fanciful name of Althea. Her husband, in a fit of petulance at some exceptional density of vision, had once told her that her name should have been Jane—Jane, Maud, Amy, any of those old-fashioned, early Victorian names would have suited Althea, and Althea's outlook on life when she had married Perceval Scrope.

Althea's drawing-room attained beauty, not only because of its proportions, and its delightful outlook on St. James's Park, but also because quite a number of highly intelligent people had seen to it that it should be beautiful.

Although Scrope, who thought he knew his young wife so well, would have been surprised and perhaps a little piqued if he had been told it, Althea preferred the house as it had been before her marriage, in the days when it was scarcely furnished, when this room, for instance, had been the library-smoking-room of its owner, an owner too poor to offer himself any of the luxurious fitments which had been added to make it suitable for his rich bride.

As soon as Scrope's engagement to the provincial heiress Althea then was had been announced, his friends—and he was a man of many friends—had delighted to render him the service of making the pleasant old house in Delahay Street look as it perchance had looked eighty or a hundred years ago. The illusion was almost perfect, so cleverly had the flotsam of Perceval Scrope's ancestral possessions been wedded to the jetsam gathered in curiosity shops and at country auctions—for the devotion of Scrope's friends had gone even to that length.

This being so, it really seemed a pity that these same kind folk had not been able to—oh! no, not *buy*, that is an ugly word, and besides it had been Perceval who had been bought, not Althea—to acquire for Scrope a wife who would have suited the house as well as the house suited Scrope.

But that had not been possible.

Even as it was, the matter of marrying their friend had not been easy. Scrope was so wilful—that was why they loved him! He had barred—absolutely barred—Americans, and that although everybody knows how useful an American heiress can be, not only with her money, but with her brightness and her wits, to an English politician. He had also stipulated for a country girl, and he would have preferred one straight out of the school-room.

Almost all his conditions had been fulfilled. Althea was nineteen at the time of her marriage, and, if not exactly country-bred—she was the only child of a Newcastle magnate—she had seen nothing of the world to which Scrope and Scrope's Egeria, the woman who had actually picked out Althea to be Scrope's wife, had introduced her.

Scrope's Egeria? At the time my little story opens, Althea had long given up being jealous—jealous, that is, in the intolerant, passionate sense of the word; in fact, she was ashamed that she had ever been so, for she now felt sure that Perceval would not have liked her, Althea, any better, even if there had not been another woman to whom he turned for flattery and sympathy.

The old ambiguous term was, in this case, no pseudonym for another and more natural, if uglier, relationship on the part of a married man, and of a man whom the careless public believed to be on exceptionally good terms with his young wife.

Scrope's Egeria was twenty-four years older than Althea, and nine years older than Scrope himself. Unfortunately she had a husband who, unlike Althea, had the bad taste, the foolishness, to be jealous of her close friendship with Perceval Scrope. And yet, while admitting to herself the man's folly, Althea had a curious liking for Egeria's husband. There was, in fact, more between them than their common interest in the other couple; for he, like Althea, provided what old-fashioned people used to call the wherewithal; he, like Althea, had been married because of the gifts he had brought in his hands, the gifts not only of that material comfort which counts for so much nowadays, but those which, to Scrope's Egeria, counted far more than luxury, that is, beauty of surroundings and refinement of living.

Mr. and Mrs. Panfillen—to give Egeria and her husband their proper names—lived quite close to Althea and Perceval Scrope, for they dwelt in Old Queen Street, within little more than a stone's throw of Delahay Street.

Joan Panfillen, unlike Althea Scrope, was exquisitely suited to her curious, old-world dwelling. She had about her small, graceful person, her picturesque and dateless dress, even in her low melodious voice, that harmony which is, to the man capable of appreciating it, the most desirable and perhaps the rarest of feminine attributes.

There was one thing which Althea greatly envied Mrs. Panfillen, and that was nothing personal to herself; it was simply the tiny formal garden which divided the house in Old Queen Street from Birdcage Walk. This garden looked fresher and greener than its fellows because, by Mrs. Panfillen's care, the miniature parterres were constantly tended and watered, while the shrubs both summer and winter were washed and cleansed as carefully as was everything else likely to be brought in contact with their owner's wife.

In spite of the fact that they lived so very near to one another, the two women were not much together, and as a rule they only met, but that was, of course, very often, when out in the political and social worlds to which they both belonged.

Althea had a curious shrinking from the Panfillens' charming house. It was there, within a very few weeks of her father's death, that she had first met Perceval Scrope—and there that he had conducted his careless wooing. It was in Mrs. Panfillen's boudoir, an octagon-shaped room on the park side of the house, that he had actually made his proposal, and that Althea, believing herself to be "in love," and uplifted by the solemn and yet joyful thought of how happy such a marriage—her marriage to a member of the first Fair Food Cabinet—would have made her father, had accepted him.

From Old Queen Street also had taken place her wedding, which, if nominally quiet, because the bride still chose to consider herself in deep mourning, had filled St. Margaret's with one of those gatherings only brought together on such an occasion—a gathering in which the foemen of yesterday, and the enemies of to-morrow, unite with the friends of to-day in order to do honour to a fellow-politician.

Althea had darker memories connected with Mrs. Panfillen's house. She had spent there, immediately after her honeymoon, an unhappy fortnight, waiting for the workpeople to leave her future home in Delahay Street. It was during that fortnight that for the first time her girlish complacency had forsaken her, and she had been made to understand how inadequate her husband found her to the position she was now called upon to fill. It was then that there had first come to her the humiliating suspicion that her bridegroom could not forgive her his own sale of himself. Scrope and Joan Panfillen were subtle people, living in a world of subtleties, yet in this subtle, unspoken matter of Scrope's self-contempt concerning his marriage, the simple Althea's knowledge far preceded theirs.

In those days Joan Panfillen, kindest, most loyal of hostesses, had always been taking the bride's part, but how unkind—yes, unkind was the word—Perceval was, even then!

Althea had never forgotten one little incident connected with that time, and this afternoon she suddenly remembered it with singular vividness. Scrope had been caricatured in *Punch* as Scrooge; and—well—Althea had not quite understood.

"Good Lord!" he had exclaimed, turning to the older woman, "Althea doesn't know who Scrooge was!" and quickly he had proceeded to put his young wife through a sharp, and to her a very bewildering examination, concerning people and places some of whom she had never heard of, while others seemed vaguely, worryingly familiar. He had ended up with the words, "And I suppose you consider yourself educated!" A chance muttered word had then told her that none of these places were real—that none of these people Perceval had spoken of with such intimate knowledge, had ever lived!

Althea had felt bitterly angered as well as hurt. Tears had welled up into her brown eyes; and Mrs. Panfillen, intervening with far more eager decision than she generally showed about even important matters, had cried, "That's not fair! In fact you are being quite absurd, Perceval! I've never cared for Dickens, and I'm sure most people, at any rate most women, who say they like him are pretending—pretending all the time! I don't believe there's a girl in London who could answer the questions you put to Althea just now, and if there is such a girl then she's a literary monster, and I for one don't want to know her."

As only answer Scrope had turned and put a thin brown finger under Althea's chin. "Crying?" he had said, "Baby! She shan't be made to learn her Dickens if she doesn't want to, so there!"

At the time Althea had tried to smile, but the words her husband had used had hurt her, horribly, for they had seemed to cast a reflection on her father—the father who thought so much of education, and who had been at such pains to obtain for his motherless only child an ideal chaperon-governess, a lady who had always lived with the best families in Newcastle. Miss Burt would certainly have made her pupil read Dickens if Dickens were in any real sense an educating influence, instead of writing, as Althea had always understood he did, only about queer and vulgar people.

Not educated? Why, her father had sent her away from him for a whole year to Dresden, in order that she might learn German and study music to the best possible advantage! True, she had not learnt her French in France, for her father had a prejudice against the French; he belonged to a generation which admired Germany, and disliked and distrusted the French. She had, however, been taught French by an excellent teacher, a French Protestant lady who had lived all her life in England. Of course Althea had never read a French novel, but she could recite, even now, whole pages of Racine and Corneille by heart.

And yet, even in this matter of languages, Perceval was unfair, for some weeks after he had said that cruel thing to her about education, and when they were at last settling down in their own house, arranging the details of their first dinner party, he had said to her with a certain abrupt ill-humour, "The one language I thought you *did* know was menu-French!"

Joan Panfillen was also disappointed in Althea. Scrope's Egeria had hoped to convert Scrope's wife, not into a likeness of herself—she was far too clever a woman to hope to do that—but into a bright, cheerful companion for Perceval Scrope's lighter hours. She had always vaguely supposed that this was the rôle reserved to pretty, healthy young women possessed of regular features, wavy brown hair, and good teeth....

But Mrs. Panfillen had soon realised, and the knowledge brought with it much unease and pain, that she had made a serious mistake in bringing about the marriage. And yet it had been necessary to do something; there had come a moment when not only she, but even Scrope himself, had felt that he must be lifted out of the class—always distrusted and despised in England—of political adventurers. Scrope required, more than most men, the solid platform, nay, the pedestal, of wealth, and accordingly his Egeria had sacrificed herself and, incidentally, the heiress, Althea.

But, as so often happens to those who make the great renouncement, Joan Panfillen found that after all no such thing as true sacrifice was to be required of her.

After his marriage, Scrope was more often with her than he had ever been, and far more willing, not only to ask but to take, his Egeria's advice on all that concerned his brilliant, meteoric career. He seldom mentioned his wife, but Mrs. Panfillen knew her friend far too well not to know how it was with him; Althea fretted his nerves, offended his taste, jarred his conscience, at every turn of their joint life.

There were, however, two meagre things to the good—Althea's fortune, the five thousand a year, which now, after four years, did not seem so large an income as it had seemed at first; and the fact that Scrope's marriage had extinguished the odious, and, what was much more unpleasant to such a woman as was Joan Panfillen, the ridiculous, jealousy of Joan's husband.

Thomas Panfillen greatly admired Althea; he thought her what she was—a very lovely young woman, and the fact that he had known her father made him complacently suppose that he had brought about her marriage to the peculiar, he was told the remarkably clever, if rather odd, Perceval Scrope.

Baulked of certain instinctive rights, the human heart seeks compensation as surely as water seeks its level. Althea, unknown to herself, had a compensation. His name was John Bustard. He was in a public office—to be precise, the Privy Council Office. He lived in rooms not far from his work, that is, not far from Delahay Street, and he had got into the way of dropping in to tea two, three, sometimes even four times a week.

The fact that Bustard was an old schoolfellow of Scrope's had been his introduction to Althea in the early days when she had been conscientiously anxious to associate herself with her husband's interests past and present. But of the innumerable people with whom Scrope had brought her into temporary contact, Mr. Bustard—she always called him Mr. Bustard, as did most other people—was the one human being who, being the fittest as regarded herself, survived.

And yet never had there been a man less suited to play the part of hero, or even of consoler. Mr. Bustard was short, and his figure was many years older than his age, which was thirty-four. While forcing himself to take two constitutionals a day, he indulged in no other manlier form of exercise, and his contempt for golf was the only thing that tended to a lack of perfect understanding between his colleagues and himself. He was interested in his work, but he tried to forget it when he was not at the office. Bustard was a simple soul, but blessed with an unformulated, though none the less real, philosophy of life.

Of the matter nearest his heart he scarcely ever spoke, partly because he had always supposed it to be uninteresting to anyone but himself, and also on account of a certain thorny pride which prevented his being willing to ask favours from the indifferent.

This matter nearest Mr. Bustard's heart concerned his two younger brothers and an orphan sister whom he supremely desired to do the best for, and to set well forward in life.

It was of these three young people that he and Althea almost always talked, and if Althea allowed herself to have an ardent wish, it was that her husband would permit her to invite Mr. Bustard's sister for a few weeks when the girl left the German finishing school which she and Mr. Bustard had chosen, after much anxious deliberation, a year before.

It soothed Althea's sore heart to know that there was at least one person in her husband's circle who thought well of her judgment, who trusted in her discretion, and who did her the compliment of not only asking, but also of taking her advice.

John Bustard had formed a very good opinion of Althea, and, constitutionally incapable of divining the causes which had determined the choice of Scrope's wife, he considered Mrs. Scrope a further proof, if indeed proof were needed, of his brilliant schoolfellow's acute intelligence. He had ventured to say as much to Scrope's late official chief, one of the few men to whom Mr. Bustard, without a sufficient cause, would have mentioned a lady's name. But he had been taken aback, rather disturbed, by the old statesman's dry comment: "Ay, there's always been method in Scrope's madness. I agree that he has made, from his own point of view, a very good marriage."

His wife's friendship with Mr. Bustard did not escape Perceval Scrope's ironic notice. He affected to think his old schoolfellow a typical member of the British public, and he had nicknamed him "the Bullometer," but, finding that his little joke vexed Althea, he had, with unusual consideration, dropped it.

Unfortunately the one offensive epithet was soon exchanged for another; in allusion doubtless to some historical personage of whom Althea had no knowledge, Scrope began to call Bustard her fat friend. "How's your fat friend?" he would ask, and a feeling of resentment filled Althea's breast. It was not John Bustard's fault that he had a bad figure; it was caused by the sedentary nature of his work, and because, instead of spending his salary in the way most civil servants spend theirs, that is in selfish amusements, he spent it on his younger brothers, and on his little sister's education.

Althea again went over to the window and looked out. It had now left off snowing, and the mists were gathering over the park. Soon a veil of fog would shut out the still landscape. If Mr. Bustard were coming this afternoon she hoped he would come soon, and so be gone before Perceval came in.

Perceval was going to make a great speech in the House to-night, and Althea was rather ashamed that she did not care more. He had been put up to speak against those who had once been of his own political household and who now regarded him as a renegade, but the subject was one sure to inspire him, for it was that which he had made his own, and which had led to his secession from his party. Althea and Mrs. Panfillen were going together to hear the speech, but, to his wife's surprise, Scrope had refused to dine with the Panfillens that same evening.

Perceval Scrope had not been well. To his vexation the fact had been mentioned in the papers. The intense cold had tried him—the cold, and a sudden visit to his constituency.

Althea could not help feeling slightly contemptuous of Perceval's physical delicacy. Her husband had often looked ill lately, not as ill as people told her he looked, but still very far from well. Only to herself did Althea say what she felt sure was the truth, namely that Perceval's state was due to himself, due to his constant rushing about, to the way in which he persistently over-excited himself; last, but by no means least, to the way he ate and drank when the food and drink pleased him.

Althea judged her husband with the clear, pitiless eyes of youth, but none of those about her knew that she so judged him. Indeed, there were some in her circle, kindly amiable folk, who believed, and said perhaps a little too loudly, that Althea was devoted to Perceval, and that their marriage was one of those delightful unions which are indeed made in Heaven....

From the further corner of the room there came the sharp ring of the telephone bell. No doubt a message saying that Perceval had altered his plans and was dining out, alone.

Insensibly Althea's lips tightened. She thought she knew what her husband was about to suggest. She felt sure that he would tell her, as he had told her so many times before when he had failed her, to offer herself to Mrs. Panfillen for dinner.

But no—the voice she heard calling her by name was not that of Perceval Scrope. It was a woman's voice, and it seemed to float towards her from a far distance. "Althea," called the strange voice, "Althea."

"Yes?" she said, "who is it? I can hardly hear you," and then, with startling closeness and clearness—the telephone plays one such tricks—came the answer in a voice she knew well, "It is I—Joan Panfillen! Are you alone, Althea? Yes? Ah! that's good! I want you to do me a kindness, dear. I want you to come round here now—at once. Don't tell anyone you are coming to me. I have a reason for this. Can you hear what I say, Althea?"

"Yes," said the listener hesitatingly, "yes, I hear you quite well now, Joan."

"Come in by the park side, I mean through the garden—the gate is unlocked, and I will let you in by the window. Be careful as you walk across the flags, it's very slippery to-night. Can you come now, at once?"

Althea hesitated a moment. Then she answered, in her low, even voice, "Yes, I'll come now, at once."

A kindness? What kindness could she, Althea Scrope, do Joan Panfillen? The fear of the other woman, the hidden distrust with which she regarded her, gathered sudden force. Not lately, but in the early days of Scrope's marriage, Mrs. Panfillen had more than once tried to use her friend's wife, believing—strange that she should have made such a mistake—that Althea might succeed where she herself had failed in persuading Scrope for his own good. Althea now told herself that no doubt Joan wished to see her on some matter connected with Perceval's coming speech.

As this thought came to her Althea's white forehead wrinkled in vexed thought. It was too bad that she should have to go out now, when she was expecting Mr. Bustard, to whom she had one or two rather important things to say about his sister——But stay, why should he be told that she was out? Why indeed should she be still out when Mr. Bustard did come? It was not yet five o'clock, and he seldom came before a quarter past. With luck she might easily go over to Joan Panfillen's house and be back before he came.

Althea walked quickly out of the drawing-room and down into the hall. Her fur cloak had been carefully hung up as she had directed. Perceval always said Luke was a stupid servant, but she liked Luke; he was careful, honest, conscientious, a very different type of man from the butler, Dockett.

Althea passed out into the chilly, foggy air. Delahay Street, composed of a few high houses, looked dark, forbidding, deserted. She had often secretly wondered why her husband chose to live in such a place. Of course she knew that their friends raved about the park side of the house, but the wife of Perceval Scrope scarcely ever went in or out of her own door without remembering a dictum of her father's: "Nothing makes up for a good front entrance."

Althea walked quickly towards Great George Street; to the left she passed Boar's Head Yard, where lived an old cabman in whom she took an interest, and whose cab generally stood at Storey's Gate.

How strange to think that here had once stood Oliver Cromwell's house! Her husband had told her this fact very soon after their marriage; it had seemed to please him very much that they lived so near the spot where Cromwell had once lived. Althea even at the time had thought this pleasure odd, in fact affected, on Perceval's part.

If the great Protector's house stood there *now*, filled with interesting little relics of the man, she could have understood, perhaps to a certain extent sympathised with, Perceval's feeling, for Cromwell had been one of her father's heroes. But to care or pretend to care for a vanished association——!

But Perceval was like that. No man living—or so Althea believed—was so full of strange whimsies and fads as was Perceval Scrope! And so thinking of him she suddenly remembered, with a tightening of the heart, how often her husband's feet had trodden the way she was now treading, hastening from the house which she had just left to the house to which she was now going.

Jealous of Joan Panfillen? Nay, Althea assured herself that there was no room in her heart for jealousy, but it was painful, even more, it was hateful, to know that there were people who pitied her because of this peculiar intimacy between Perceval and Joan. Why, quite lately, there had been a recrudescence of talk about their friendship, so an ill-bred busybody had hinted to Althea only the day before.

The wife was dimly aware that there had been a time when Mrs. Panfillen had hoped to form with her an unspoken compact; each would have helped the other, that is, to "manage" Perceval; but the moment when such an alliance would have been possible had now gone for ever—even if it had ever existed. Althea would have had to have been a different woman,—older, cleverer, less scrupulous, more indifferent than she was, even now, to the man she had married, to make such a compact possible.

When about to cross Great George Street she stopped and hesitated. Why should she do this thing, why leave her house at Joan Panfillen's bidding? But Althea, even as she hesitated, knew that she would go on. She had said that she was coming, and she was not one to break lightly even a light word.

As she crossed Storey's Gate, she noticed the stationary cab of the old man who lived in Boar's Head Yard. It had been standing there when she had come in from her walk, and she felt a thrill of pity—the old man made a gallant fight against misfortune. She and Joan Panfillen were both very kind to him.

Althea told herself that this sad world is full of real trouble, and the thought made her ashamed of the feelings which she had just allowed to possess and shake her with jealous pain. And yet—yet, though many people envied her, how far from happy Althea knew herself to be, and how terribly grey her life now looked, stretching out in front of her.

As she passed into Birdcage Walk, and came close to the little iron gate which Mrs. Panfillen had told her was unlocked, she saw that a woman stood on the path of the tiny garden behind the railings.

Of course it was not Joan herself; the thought that Joan, delicate, fragile as she was, would come out into the cold, foggy air was unthinkable; scarcely less strange was it to see standing there, cloakless and hatless, Joan's maid, a tall, gaunt, grey-haired woman named Bolt, who in the long ago had been nurse to the Panfillens' dead child. Scrope had told Althea the story of the brief tragedy very early in his acquaintance with her; he had spoken with strong feeling, and that although the child had been born, had lived, and had died before he himself had known Joan.

In the days when she had been Mrs. Panfillen's guest, that is before her marriage, Althea had known the maid well, known and liked her grim honesty of manner, but since Althea's marriage to Perceval Scrope there had come a change over Bolt's manner. She also had made Althea feel that she was an interloper, and now the sight of the woman standing waiting in the cold mist disturbed her.

Bolt looked as if she had been there a very long time, and yet Althea had hurried; she was even a little breathless. As she touched the gate, she saw that it swung loosely. Everything had been done to make her coming easy; how urgent must be Joan's need of her!

Althea became oppressed with a vague fear. She looked at the maid questioningly. "Is Mrs. Panfillen ill?" she asked. The other shook her head. "There's nothing ailing Mrs. Panfillen," she said in a low voice.

Together, quite silently, they traversed the flagged path, and then Bolt did a curious thing. She preceded her mistress's visitor up the iron steps leading to the boudoir window, and leaving her there, on the little balcony, went down again into the garden, and once more took up her station near the gate as if mounting guard.

The long French window giving access to the boudoir was closed, and in the moment that elapsed before it was opened from within Althea Scrope took unconscious note of the room she knew so well, and of everything in it, including the figure of the woman she had come to see.

It was a panelled octagon, the panels painted a pale Wedgwood blue, while just below the ceiling concave medallions were embossed with flower garlands and amorini.

A curious change had been made since Althea had last seen the room. An old six-leaved screen, of gold so faded as to have become almost silver in tint, which had masked the door, now stood exactly opposite the window behind which Althea was standing. It concealed the straight Empire sofa which, as Mr. Panfillen was fond of telling his wife's friends, on the very rare occasions when he found himself in this room with one of them, had formerly stood in the Empress Josephine's boudoir at Malmaison; and, owing to the way it was now placed, the old screen formed a delicate and charming background to Mrs. Panfillen's figure.

Scrope's Egeria stood in the middle of the room waiting for Scrope's wife. She was leaning forward in a curious attitude, as if she were listening, and the lemon-coloured shade of the lamp standing on the table threw a strange gleam on her lavender silk gown, fashioned, as were ever the clothes worn by Joan Panfillen, with a certain austere simplicity and disregard of passing fashion.

Althea tapped at the window, and the woman who had sent for her turned round, and, stepping forward, opened the window wide.

"Come in!" she cried. "Come in, Althea—how strange that you had to knock! I've been waiting for you so long."

"I came as quickly as I could—I don't think I can have been five minutes."

Althea stepped through the window, bringing with her a blast of cold, damp air. She looked questioningly at Mrs. Panfillen. She felt, she hardly knew why, trapped. The other's look of anxious, excited scrutiny disturbed her.

Mrs. Panfillen's fair face, usually pale, was flushed.

So had she reddened, suddenly, when Althea had come to tell her of her engagement to Perceval Scrope. So had she looked when standing on the doorstep as Althea and Perceval started for their honeymoon, just after there had taken place a strange little scene—for Scrope, following the example of Thomas Panfillen, who had insisted on what he called saluting the bride, had taken Panfillen's wife into his arms and kissed her.

"Althea"—Joan took the younger woman's hand in hers and held it, closely, as she spoke, "don't be frightened,—but Perceval is here, ill,—and I've sent for you to take him home."

"Ill?" A look of dismay came over Althea's face. "I hope he's not too ill to speak to-night—that would be dreadful—he'd be terribly upset, terribly disappointed!" Even as she spoke she knew she was using words which to the other would seem exaggerated, a little childish.

"I'm sure he'd rather you took him home, I'm sure he'd rather not be found——" Mrs. Panfillen hesitated a moment, and again she said the words "'ill', 'here'," and for the first time Althea saw that there was a look of great pain and strain on Joan's worn, sensitive face.

"Of course not!" said the young wife quickly. "Of course he mustn't be ill here; he must come home, at once."

Althea's pride was protesting hotly against her husband's stopping a moment in a house where he was not wanted—pride and a certain resentment warring together in her heart. How strange London people were! This woman whom folk—the old provincial word rose to her lips—whom folk whispered was over-fond of Perceval—why, no sooner was he ill than her one thought was how to get rid of him quietly and quickly!

Mrs. Panfillen, looking at her, watching with agonised intensity the slow workings of Althea's mind, saw quite clearly what Perceval's wife was feeling, saw it with a bitter sense of what a few moments ago she would have thought inconceivable she could ever feel again—amusement.

She went across to the window and opened it. As if in answer to a signal, the little iron gate below swung widely open: "Bolt has gone to get a cab," she said, without turning round; "we thought that it would be simplest. The old cabman knows us all—it will be quicker." She spoke breathlessly, but there was a tone of decision in her voice, a gentle restrained tone, but one which Althea knew well to spell finality.

"But where *is* Perceval?"

Althea looked round her bewildered. She noticed, for the first time, that flung carelessly across two chairs lay his outdoor coat, his gloves, his stick, his hat. Then he also had come in by the park side of the house?

Mrs. Panfillen went towards her with slow, hesitating steps.

"He is here," she said in a low tone, "behind the screen. He was sitting on the sofa reading me the notes of his speech, and—and he fell back." She began moving the screen, and as she did so she went on, "I sent for Bolt—

she was a nurse once, you know, and she got the brandy which you see there———"

But Althea hardly heard the words; she was gazing, with an oppressed sense of discomfort and fear, at her husband. Yes, Perceval looked ill—very ill,—and he was lying in so peculiar a position! "I suppose when people faint they have to put them like that," thought Althea to herself, but she felt concerned, a little frightened....

Perceval Scrope lay stretched out stiffly on the sofa, his feet resting on a chair which had been placed at the end of the short, frail-looking little couch. His fair, almost lint white, hair was pushed back from his forehead, showing its unusual breadth. The grey eyes were half closed, and he was still wearing, wound about his neck so loosely that it hid his mouth and chin, a silk muffler.

Althea had the painful sensation that he did not like her to be there, that it must be acutely disagreeable to him to feel that she saw him in such a condition of helplessness and unease. And yet she went on looking at him, strangely impressed, not so much by the rigidity, as by the intense stillness of his body. Scrope as a rule was never still; when he was speaking, his whole body, each of his limbs, spoke with him.

By the side of the sofa was a small table, on which stood a decanter, unstoppered.

"Has he been like that long?" Althea whispered at length. "He—he looks so strange."

Joan Panfillen came close up to the younger woman; again she put her hand on her companion's arm.

"Althea," she said, "don't you understand? Can't you see the dreadful thing that has happened?"—and as the other looked down into the quivering face turned up to hers, she added with sudden passion, "Should I want you to take him away if he were still here?—should I want him to go if there were anything left that I could do for him?"

And then Althea at last understood, and so understanding her mind for once moved quickly, and she saw with mingled terror and revolt what it was that the woman on whose face her eyes were now riveted was requiring of her.

"You sent for me to take him home—dead?"

It was a statement rather than a question. Mrs. Panfillen made a scarcely perceptible movement of assent. "It is what he would have wished," she whispered, "I am quite sure it is what he would have wished you to do."

"I—I am sorry, but I don't think I can do that."

Althea was speaking to herself rather than to the other woman. She was grappling with a feeling of mortal horror and fear. She had always been afraid of Perceval Scrope, afraid and yet fascinated, and now he, dead, seemed to be even more formidable, more beckoning, than he had been alive.

She turned away and covered her eyes with her hand. "Why did you tell me?" she asked, a little wildly. "If you hadn't told me that he was dead I should never have known. I should even have done the—the dreadful thing you want me to do."

"Bolt thought that—Bolt said you would not know," Mrs. Panfillen spoke with sombre energy. "She wished me to allow her to take him down into the garden to meet you in the darkness——But,—but Althea, that would have been an infamous thing from me to you——" She waited a moment, and then in a very different voice, in her own usual measured and gentle accents, she added, "My dear, forgive me. We will never speak of this again. I was wrong, selfish, to think of subjecting you to such an ordeal. All I ask"—and there came into her tone a sound of shamed pleading—"is that you should allow Tom—Tom and other people—to think that you were here when it happened."

Althea remained silent. Then, uncertainly, she walked across to the window and opened it. The action was symbolic—and so it was understood by the woman watching her so anxiously.

But still Althea said nothing. She stood looking out into the darkness, welcoming the feel of the cold damp air. She gave herself a few brief moments—they seemed very long moments to Joan Panfillen—before she said the irrevocable words, and when she did say them, they sounded muffled, and uttered from far away, for Althea as she spoke did not turn round; she feared to look again on that which might unnerve her, render her unfit for what she was about to do.

"Joan," she said, "I will do what you ask. You were right just now—right, I mean, in telling me what Perceval would have wished."

She spoke with nervous, dry haste, and, to her relief, the other woman spared her thanks....

There was a long silence, and then Mrs. Panfillen crept up close to Althea and touched her, making her start violently. "Then I will call Bolt," she said, and made as if to pass through the window, but Althea stopped her with a quick movement of recoil—"No, no!" she cried, "let me do that!" and she ran down the iron steps; it was good to be out of sight even for a moment of the still presence of the dead—the dead whose mocking spirit seemed to be still terribly alive.

But during the long, difficult minutes that followed, it was Joan Panfillen, not Althea Scrope, who shrank and blenched. It was Althea who put out her young strength to help to lift the dead man, and, under cover of the sheltering mist, to make the leaden feet retrace their steps down the iron stairway, and along the narrow path they had so often leapt up and along with eager haste.

To two of the three women the progress seemed intolerably slow, but to Althea it was all too swift; she dreaded with an awful dread the companioned drive which lay before her.

Perhaps something of what she was feeling was divined by Mrs. Panfillen, for at the very last Scrope's Egeria forgot self, and made, in all sincerity, an offer which on her part was heroic.

"Shall I come with you?" she whispered, averting her eyes from that which lay huddled up by Althea's side, "I will come, willingly; let me come—Althea."

But Althea only shook her head in cold, hurried refusal. She felt that with speech would go a measure of her courage.

Afterwards Althea remembered that there had come a respite,—what had seemed to her at the time an inexplicable delay. A man and a girl had gone slowly by, staring curiously at the two bare-headed women standing out on the pavement, and on whose pale faces there fell the quivering gleam of the old-fashioned cab lamp. Then, when the footfalls of these passers-by had become faint, Bolt spoke to the driver, and handed him some money. Althea heard the words as in dream, "Get along as quick as you can to 24, Delahay Street, there's a good man," and then the clink of silver in the stillness, followed by the full sound of the man's wheezy gratitude.

There came a sudden movement and the dread drive began, the horse slipping, the cab swaying and jolting over the frozen ground.

With a gesture which was wholly instinctive, Althea put out her arm,—her firm, rounded, living arm,—and slipped it round the inert, sagging thing which had been till an hour ago Perceval Scrope. And, as she did so, as she pressed him to her, and kept from him the ignominy of physical helplessness, there came a great lightening of her spirit.

Fear, the base fear bred of the imagination, fell away from her. For the first time there came the certainty that her husband was at last satisfied with her; for the first time she was able to do Perceval Scrope dead what she had never been able to do Perceval Scrope alive, a great service—a service which she might have refused to do.

Once or twice, very early in their married life, Perceval had praised her, and his praise had given Althea exquisite pleasure because it was so rare, so seldom lavished; and this long-lost feeling of joy in her husband's approval came back, filling her eyes with tears. Now at last Althea felt as if she and Perceval Scrope were one, fused in that kindly sympathy and understanding which, being the manner of woman she was, Althea supposed to be the very essence of conjugal love.

As they were clasped together, she, the quick, he, the dead, Althea lost count of time; it might have been a moment, it might have been an hour, when at last the jolting ceased.

As the old man got off the box of his cab, and rang the bell, Big Ben boomed out the quarter-past five.

Since she had last gone through that door a yawning gap had come in Althea's life, a gap which she had herself bridged. Fear had dropped from her; she could never again be afraid as she had been afraid when she, Joan and Perceval had formed for the last time a trinity. The feeling which had so upheld her, the feeling that for the first time she and her husband were in unison, gave her not only courage but serenity of spirit. Althea shrank from acting a lie, but she saw, for the first time, through Perceval Scrope's eyes, and she admitted the necessity.

As the door opened, she remembered, almost with exultation, that Dockett, the butler, was out, and that it was only with Luke, the slow young footman, that she would have to deal. As she saw his tall, thin figure emerge hesitatingly into the street, Mrs. Scrope called out in a strong, confident voice, "Luke—come here! Help me to get Mr. Scrope indoors. He is ill; and as soon as we have got him into the morning room, you must go off for a doctor, at once——"

She waved aside the cabman almost impatiently, and it was Althea, Althea helped by Luke, who carried Perceval Scrope over the threshold of his own house, and so into a small room on the ground floor, a room opening out of the hall, and looking out on to the street.

"He looks very bad, don't 'e, ma'am?" Luke was startled out of his acquired passivity. "I'd better go right off now." She bent her head.

And then Althea, again alone with the dead man, suddenly became oppressed once more with fear, not the physical terror which had possessed her when Joan Panfillen had told her the awful truth, but none the less to her a very agonising form of fear. Althea was afraid that now, when approaching the end of her ordeal, she would fail Scrope and the woman he had loved. What was she to say, what story could she invent to tell those who would come and press her with quick eager questions? She knew herself to be incapable, not only of untruth, but of invention, and yet now both were about to be required of her.

Althea turned out the lights, and wandered out into the hall. She felt horribly lonely; with the exception of the kindly, stupid youth who had now gone to find a doctor, there was not a member of her considerable household in sufficient human sympathy with her to be called to her aid.

She remembered with a pang that this question of their servants had been one of the many things concerning which there had been deep fundamental disagreement between her husband and herself. She had been accustomed to a well-ordered, decorous household, and would even have enjoyed managing such a one; but Perceval—Perceval influenced by Dockett—had ordained otherwise, and Althea had soon become uneasily aware that the order and decorum reigning below stairs were only apparent. Even now there came up from the basement the sound of loud talking, of unrestrained laughter.

Suddenly someone knocked at the door, a loud double knock which stilled, as if by magic, the murmur of the voices below.

Althea looked around her doubtfully, then she retreated into the darkened room, but no one came up, and she remembered that the other servants of course supposed Luke to be on duty. It might be—nay, it almost certainly was—the doctor. With faltering steps she again came out into the hall and opened the front door; and then, when she saw who it was who stood there, his kind honest eyes blinking in the sudden light, Althea began to cry.

The tears ran down her cheeks; she sighed convulsively, and John Bustard, looking at her with deep concern and dismay, was quite unaware—he does not know even to this day—that it was with relief.

"What is it?" he said. "My dear Mrs. Scrope—what is the matter? Would you like me to go away—or—or can I be of any use?"

"Oh, yes," she said piteously. "Indeed you can be of use. Don't go away—stay with me—I'm—I'm so frightened, Mr. Bustard. Perceval—poor Perceval is—is ill, and I'm afraid to stay in there with him."

And it was Mr. Bustard who at once took command—command of Althea, whom he ultimately ordered to bed; command of the excited household, whose excitement he sternly suppressed; it was Mr. Bustard who, believing he told truth, lied for Althea, first to the doctor, and later to the coroner.

"How fortunate it was for poor Althea that Mr. Bustard, that nice little man in the Privy Council Office, was actually in the house when poor Perceval Scrope's death took place!" bold and cruel people would say to Mrs. Panfillen, watching the while to see how she took their mention of the dead man's name.

"Yes," she would answer them quietly. "Very fortunate indeed. And it was so kind of Mr. Bustard to get his sister to go away with Althea. Poor Althea is so alone in the world. I hope she will come and stay with us when she comes back to town; we were Perceval Scrope's oldest, I might say closest, friends. You know that their marriage—his and Althea's—took place from our house?"

The only human being who scented a mystery was Dockett—Dockett, who was mindful, as he had a right to be, of his lawful perquisites, and who will never forgive himself for having been out on that fateful afternoon.

"I'd give something to know the whereabouts of Mr. Scrope's overcoat, to say nothing of his hat and stick. That common ash stick's a relic—it may be worth money some day!" he observed threateningly to the footman. But Luke, as only answer, stared at him with stolid dislike.

Luke had seen nothing of the hat and stick; no doubt they had been left in the cab in which Mr. Scrope had come back, ill, from the House. As for the overcoat, it had probably disappeared in the confusion, the hurried coming and going, of that evening when Luke had been almost run off his legs answering the door, and his head made quite giddy answering enquiries. But it was not Luke's business to say what he thought or did not think. With such a man as Mr. Dockett, it only led to unpleasantness.

II

MR. JARVICE'S WIFE

I

"About that letter of your uncle's? I take it you have no one to suggest?"

Thomas Carden glanced anxiously at the son in whom he had so strong a confidence, and who was the secret pride of his eyes, the only love of his austere, hard-working life.

The two were a great contrast to one another. The older man was short and slight, with the delicate, refined, spiritual face, so often seen in the provincial man of business belonging to that disappearing generation of Englishmen who found time to cultivate the things of the mind as well as the material interests of life. A contrast, indeed, to the tall, singularly handsome, alert-looking man whom he had just addressed, and whose perfect physical condition made him appear somewhat younger than his thirty-two years.

And yet, in spite or perhaps because of this contrast between them, the two were bound in the closest, if not exactly in the most confidential, ties of affection. And, as a matter of course, they were partners in the great metal-broking business of Josh. Carden, Thomas Carden and Son, which had been built up by three generations of astute, self-respecting citizens of Birmingham.

It was Easter Monday, and the two men were lingering over breakfast, in a way they seldom allowed themselves time to do on ordinary week-days, in the finely proportioned, book-lined dining-room of one of those spacious old houses which remain to prove that the suburb of Edgbaston was still country a hundred years ago.

Theodore Carden looked across the table meditatively. He had almost forgotten his uncle's letter, for, since that letter had been read and cursorily discussed, he and his father had been talking of a matter infinitely more important to them both. The matter in question was the son's recent engagement and coming marriage, a marriage which was a source of true satisfaction to the older man. His father's unselfish joy in the good thing which had befallen him touched Theodore Carden keenly, for the niche occupied in most men's minds by their intimate feminine circle was filled in that of the young man by the diminutive figure of the senior partner of Carden and Son.

As is perhaps more often the case than those who despise human nature believe, many have the grace to reverence and admire the qualities in which they know themselves to be deficient. Such a man was the younger Carden.

To-day the depths had been stirred, and he let his mind dwell with a certain sense of shame and self-rebuke on his own and his father's ideals of human conduct. Even as a schoolboy, Theodore had come to realise how much more he knew of the ugly side of life than did his father. But then, old Mr. Carden was quite exceptional; he knew nothing—or so at least his son believed, and loved him for it—of the temptations, conflicts, victories, and falls of the average sensual man.

Theodore's father had been engaged, at twenty, to a girl of his own age whom he had not been able to marry till twelve years later; she had left him a widower with this one child after five years of married life, and Thomas Carden, as he had himself once told his son in a moment of unwonted confidence, had been absolutely faithful to her before the marriage and since her death.

The woman—many people would have said the very fortunate young woman—who was so soon to become Mrs. Theodore Carden would not possess such a husband as Thomas Carden had been to his wife.

And yet, in his heart, Theodore was well aware that the gentle girl he loved would probably be a happier woman than his own mother had been, for he, unlike his father, in his dealings with the other sex could call up at will that facile and yet rather rare gift of tenderness which women, so life had taught him, value far more than the deeper, inarticulate love....

Carden came back to the prosaic question of his uncle's letter with a distinct effort.

"Have I anyone to suggest?" he echoed. "I have no one to suggest, father. I know, of course, exactly the sort of man Uncle Barrett is looking for; he's asking us to find him the perfect clerk every man of business has sought for at some time or other. If I were you I should write and tell him that the man he wants us to find never has to look outside England for a job, and, what is more, would rather be a clerk here—if he's any sense—than a partner in New Zealand!"

A smile quivered for a moment over the young man's shrewd face; his uncle was evidently seeking such a man as he was himself, but such men, so Theodore Carden was able to tell himself without undue conceit, were not likely to go into voluntary exile even with the bribe of eventual partnership in a flourishing business.

There was a pause, and then again the older man broke the silence with something entirely irrelevant to the subject which was filling the minds of his son and himself.

"You haven't looked at the *Post* this morning? There's nothing in it. Dearth of real news is, I suppose, responsible for this?" and he pointed, frowning as he spoke, to a column on the middle page headed "The Jarvice Mystery. New Developments."

Again a shrewd, good-humoured smile quivered on his son's firm mouth.

"In these days newspapers have to follow, not lead, the public taste. Very few people are honestly as indifferent as you are, father, to that sort of story. Now even I, who never met poor old Jarvice, cannot help wondering how he came by his death; and yet you, who knew the man———"

"I knew him," said the other with a touch of impatience, "as I know, and as you know, dozens of our fellow-townsmen."

"Never mind; you, at any rate, can put a face to the man's name; and yet the question as to whether he was or was not poisoned by his wife, is one of indifference to you! Now I submit that in this indifference you are really a little———" he hesitated for a word, but found that none so well expressed his thought as that which had first arisen to his lips—"peculiar, father."

"Am I?" said Thomas Carden slowly; "am I so, Theodore? Nay, nay, I deny that I am indifferent! Lane"—Major Lane was at that time Head Constable of Birmingham, and a lifelong friend of the speaker—"Lane was quite full of it last night. He insisted on telling me all the details of the affair, and what shocked me, my boy, was not so much the question which, of course, occupied Lane—that is, as to whether that unhappy young woman poisoned her husband or not—but the whole state of things which he disclosed about them. Lane told me certain facts concerning Jarvice, whom, as you truly say, I have known, in a sense, for years, which I should not have thought possible of any man—vile things, which should have prevented his thinking of marriage, especially of marriage with a young wife."

Theodore Carden remained silent; he never discussed unsavoury subjects with his father. Moreover, he had no liking for Major Lane, though he regarded him with considerable respect, and even with a feeling of gratitude. Some years before, the Head Constable had helped the young man out of a serious scrape, the one real scrape—so Carden was complacently able to assure himself—engendered by his systematic and habitual pursuit of women.

Even now he could not recall, without wincing, the interview he had had on that occasion with his father's friend. During that interview Carden had felt himself thoroughly condemned, and even despised, by the older man, and he had been made to feel that it was only for the sake of his father— his high-minded, unsuspicious father—that he was being saved from the public exposure of a peculiarly sordid divorce suit.

But it was in all sincerity that the young man now felt indignant with Major Lane for having distressed such a delicately spiritual soul as was Thomas Carden with the hidden details of the Jarvice story. After all, what interested the public was not the question of Jarvice's moral character, but whether a gently nurtured and attractive woman had carried through a sinister and ingenious crime, which, but for a mere accident, would have utterly defied detection.

Theodore Carden got up from the breakfast table and walked over to a circular bow window which commanded charming views of the wide sloping garden, interspersed with the streams and tiny ponds, which gave the house its name of Watermead, and which enabled old Mr. Carden to indulge himself with especial ease in his hobby of water gardening.

Standing there, the young man began wondering what he should do with himself this early spring day.

His *fiancée* had just left the quiet lodgings, which she and her mother, a clergyman's widow, had occupied in Birmingham during the last few weeks, to pay visits to relatives in the south of England. The thought of going to any of the neighbouring houses where he knew himself to be sure of a warm welcome, and where the news of his engagement would be received with boisterous congratulations, tempered in some cases with an underlying touch of regret and astonishment, filled him with repugnance.

The girl he had chosen to be his wife was absolutely different from the women who had hitherto attracted him; he reverenced as well as loved her, and hitherto Theodore Carden had never found reverence to be in any sense a corollary of passion, while he had judged women by those who were attractive to, or, as was quite as often the case, attracted by, himself.

The last few days had brought a great change in his life, and one which he meant should be permanent; and yet, in spite or perhaps because of this, as he stood staring with absent eyes into his father's charming garden, he found his mind dwelling persistently on the only one of his many amorous adventures which had left a deep, an enduring, and, it must be admitted, a most delightful mark on the tablets of his memory.

The whole thing was still so vivid to him that half-involuntarily he turned round and looked down the long room to where his old father was sitting. How amazed, above all how shocked and indignant, the man for whom he had so great an affection and respect would feel if he knew the pictures which were now floating before his son's retrospective vision!

Like most thinking human beings, Theodore Carden had not lived to his present age without being struck by the illogical way the world wags. Accordingly, he was often surprised and made humorously indignant by the curious moral standards—they had so many more than one—of the conventional people among whom it was his fate to dwell and have his social being.

Not one of the men he knew, with the exception of his father, and of those others—a small number truly—whom he believed to be sincerely, not conventionally, religious, but would have envied him the astonishing adventure which reconstituted itself so clearly before him to-day—and yet not one of them but would have been ready to condemn him for having done what he had done. Theodore Carden, however, so often tempted to kiss, never felt tempted to tell, and the story of that episode remained closely hidden, and would so remain, he told himself, to the end of his life.

What had happened had been briefly this.

One day in the previous October, Carden had taken his seat in the afternoon express which stops at Birmingham on its way from the north to Euston, or rather, having taken a leisurely survey of the train, which was, as he quickly noted, agreeably empty, he had indicated to the porter carrying his bag a carriage in which sat, alone, a singularly pretty woman.

As he afterwards had the delight of telling her, and, as he now reminded himself with a retrospective thrill of feeling, he had experienced, when his eyes first met those of the fair traveller, that incommunicable sensation, part physical, part mental, which your genuine Lothario, if an intelligent man, always welcomes with quickening pulse as a foretaste of the special zest to be attached to a coming pursuit.

Carden's instinct as to such delicate matters had seldom played him false; never less so than on this occasion, for, within an hour, he and the lovely stranger had reached that delightful stage of intimacy in which a man and woman each feels that he and she, while still having much to learn about the other, are on the verge of a complete understanding.

During the three hours' journey, Carden's travelling companion told him a great deal more about herself than he had chosen to reveal concerning his own life and affairs; he learnt, for instance, that she was the young wife of an old man, and that the old man was exceedingly jealous. Further, that she found the life she was compelled to lead "horribly boring," and that a widowed cousin, who lived near London, and from whom she had "expectations," formed a convenient excuse for occasional absences from home.

Concerning three matters of fact, however, she completely withheld her confidence, both then, in those first delicious hours of their acquaintance, and even later, when their friendship—well, why not say friendship, for Carden had felt a very strong liking as well as an over-mastering attraction for this Undine-like creature?—had become much closer.

The first and second facts which she kept closely hidden, for reasons which should perhaps have been obvious, were her surname—she confided to him that her Christian name was Pansy—and her husband's profession. The third fact which she concealed was the name of the town where she lived, and from which she appeared to be travelling that day.

The trifling incidents of that eventful October journey had become to a great extent blurred in Theodore Carden's memory, but what had followed was still extraordinarily vivid, and to-day, on this holiday morning, standing idly looking out of the window, he allowed his mind a certain retrospective licence.

From whom, so he now asked himself, had first come the suggestion that there should be no parting at Euston between himself and the strange elemental woman he found so full of unforced fascination and disarming charm?

The answer soon came echoing down the corridors of remembrance: from himself, of course. But even now the memory brought with it shame-faced triumph as he remembered her quick acquiescence, as free, as unashamed, as joyous as that of a spoilt child acclaiming an unlooked-for treat.

And, after all, what harm had there been in the whole halcyon adventure—what injury had it caused to any human being?

Carden put the husband, the fatuous old man, who had had the incredible folly to marry a girl thirty-five years younger than himself, out of court. Pansy, light-hearted, conscienceless Pansy—he always thought of her with a touch of easy tenderness—had run no risk of detection, for, as he had early discovered, she knew no one in London with the solitary exception of the old cousin who lived in Upper Norwood.

As for his own business acquaintances, he might, of course, have been seen by any of them taking about this singularly attractive woman, for the two went constantly to the theatre, and daily to one or other of the great restaurants. But what then? Excepting that she was quieter in manner, far better dressed, and incomparably prettier, Pansy might have been the wife or sister of any one of his own large circle of relations, that great Carden clan who held their heads so high in the business world of the Midlands.

Nay, nay, no risk had been run, and no one had been a penny the worse! Indeed, looking back, Theodore Carden told himself that it had been a perfect, a flawless episode; he even admitted that after all it was perhaps as well that there had been no attempt at a repetition.

And yet? And yet the young man, especially during the first few weeks which had followed that sequence of enchanting days, had often felt piqued, even a little surprised, that the heroine of his amazing adventure had not taken advantage of his earnest entreaty that she would give him the chance of meeting her again. He had left it to her to be mysterious; as for himself, he had seen no reason why he should conceal from her either his name or his business address.

Many men would not have been so frank, but Theodore Carden, too wise in feminine lore to claim an infallible knowledge of women, never remembered having made a mistake as to the moral social standing of a new feminine acquaintance.

During the few days they had been together, everything had gone to prove that Pansy was no masquerader from that under-world whose denizens always filled him with a sensation of mingled aversion and pity. He could not doubt—he never had doubted—that what she had chosen to tell him about herself and her private affairs was substantially true. No man, having heard her speak of it, could fail to understand her instinctive repulsion from the old husband to whom she had sold herself into bondage; and as human, if not perhaps quite as worthy of sympathy, was her restless longing for freedom to lead the pleasant life led by those of her more fortunate contemporaries whose doings were weekly chronicled in the society papers which seemed to form her only reading.

Once only had Carden felt for his entrancing companion the slightest touch of repugnance. He had taken her to a play in which a child played an important part, and she had suddenly so spoken as to make him realise with a shock of surprise that she was the mother of children! Yet the little remark made by her, "I wonder how my little girls are getting on," had been very natural and even womanly. Then, in answer to a muttered word or two on his part, she had explained that she preferred not to have news of her children when she was absent from home, as it only worried her; even when staying with the old cousin at Upper Norwood, she made a point of being completely free of all possible home troubles.

Hearing this gentle, placid explanation of her lack of maternal anxiety, Carden had put up his hand to his face to hide a smile; he had not been mistaken; Pansy was indeed the thorough-going little hedonist he had taken her to be. Still, it was difficult, even rather disturbing, to think of her as a mother, and as the mother of daughters.

Yet how deep an impression this unmoral, apparently soulless woman had made on his mind and on his emotional memory! Even now, when he had no desire, and, above all, must not allow himself to have any desire, ever to see her again, Theodore Carden felt, almost as keenly as he had done during the period of their brief intimacy, a morbid curiosity to know where she lived and had her being.

It was late in the afternoon of Easter Monday.

Theodore Carden had just come in from a long walk, and, as he passed through the circular hall around which Watermead was built, he heard the low sound of voices, those of his father and some other man, issuing from the square drawing-room always occupied by the father and son on such idle days as these. He stayed his steps, realised that the visitor was Major Lane, and then made up his mind to go up and change, instead of going straight in to his father, as he would have done had the latter been alone.

As he came down again, and crossed the now lighted hall, he met the parlour-maid, an elderly woman who had been in Thomas Carden's service ever since his wife's death. "I wonder if I can take in the lamps now, Mr. Theodore? It's getting so dark, sir."

There was a troubled sound in her voice, and the young man stopped and looked at her with some surprise.

"Of course you can, Kate," he said quickly, "why not? Why haven't you taken them in before?"

"I did go in with them half an hour ago, sir, but the master told me to take them out again. There's firelight, to be sure, and it's only Major Lane in there, but he's been here since three o'clock, and master's not had his tea yet. I suppose they thought they'd wait till you came in."

"Oh! well, if my father prefers to sit in the dark, and to put off tea till he can have my company, you had better wait till I ring, and then bring in the lamps and the tea together."

He spoke with his usual light good-nature, and passed on into the room which was the only apartment in the large old house clearly associated in his mind with the graceful, visionary figure of his dead mother.

Thomas Carden and the Head Constable were sitting in the twilight, one on each side of the fireplace, and when the young man came in, they both stirred perceptibly, and abruptly stopped speaking.

Theodore came forward and stood on the hearth-rug. "May Kate bring in the lamps, father?"

"Yes, yes, I suppose so."

And the lamps were brought in. Then came the tea-tray, placed by Kate on a large table many paces from the fire; womanless Watermead was lacking in the small elegancies of modern life, but now that would soon be remedied, so the younger Carden told himself with a slight, happy smile.

Very deliberately, and asking no questions as to milk or sugar, for well he knew the tastes of his father and of his father's friend, he poured out two cups of tea, and turning, advanced, a cup balanced in each steady hand.

But halfway up the room he stopped for a moment, arrested by the sound of his father's voice—

"Theo, my boy, I want to ask you something."

The mode of address had become of late years a little unusual, and there was a note in Thomas Carden's accents which struck his son as significant—even as solemn.

"Yes, father?"

"Did you not tell me this morning that you had never met Jarvice?"

The one onlooker, hatchet-faced Major Lane, suddenly leaned a little forward.

He was astonished at his old friend's extraordinary and uncalled-for courage, and it was with an effort, with the feeling that he was bracing himself to see something terrible take place, that he looked straight at the tall, fine-looking man who had now advanced into the circle of light thrown by the massive Argand lamps.

But Theodore Carden appeared quite unmoved, nay more, quite unconcerned, by his father's question.

"Yes," he said, "I did tell you so. I suppose I knew the old fellow by sight, but I certainly was never introduced to him. Are there any new developments?"

He turned to Major Lane with a certain curiosity, and then quite composedly handed him the cup of tea he held in his right hand.

"Well, yes," answered the other coldly, "there are several new developments. We arrested Mrs. Jarvice this morning."

"That seems rather a strong step to have taken, unless new evidence has turned up since Saturday," said Theodore thoughtfully.

"Such new evidence has come to hand since Saturday," observed Major Lane drily.

There was a pause, and again Thomas Carden addressed his son with that strange touch of solemnity, and again Major Lane, with an inward wincing, stared fixedly at the young man now standing on the hearth-rug, a stalwart, *debonair* figure, between himself and his old friend.

"Can you assure me—can you assure us both—that you never met Mrs. Jarvice?"

Carden looked down at his father with a puzzled expression.

"Of course I can't assure you of anything of the kind," he said, still speaking quite placidly. "I may have met her somewhere or other, but I can't remember having done so; and I think I should have remembered it, both because the name is an uncommon one, and because"—he turned to Major Lane—"isn't she said to be an extraordinarily pretty woman?"

As the last words were being uttered an odd thing happened. Thomas Carden suddenly dropped the cup he was holding in his hand; it rang against the brass fender and broke in several pieces, while the spoon went clattering into the fireplace.

"Father!" exclaimed Theodore, and then quickly he added, "Don't trouble to do that," for the old man was stooping over the rug, and fumbling with the broken pieces. But Thomas Carden shook his head; it was evident that he was, for the moment, physically incapable of speech.

A great fear came into the son's mind; he turned to Major Lane, and muttered in an urgent, agonised whisper, "Is it—can it be a seizure? Hadn't I better go and try to find Dr. Curle?"

But the other, with a dubious expression on his face, shook his head. "No, no," he said; "it's nothing of the kind. Your father's getting older, Carden, as we all are, and I've had to speak to him to-day about a very disagreeable matter."

He looked fixedly, probingly, at the young man.

"I think it's thoroughly upset him." The speaker hesitated, and then added: "I daresay he'll tell you about it; in any case, I'd better go now and come back later. If you can spare me half an hour this evening, I should like to have a talk with you—about the same matter."

During the last few moments Major Lane had made up his mind to take a certain course, even to run a certain risk, and that not for the first time that day, for he had already set his own intimate knowledge of Thomas Carden, the lifelong friend whose condition now wrung him with pity, against what was, perhaps, his official duty.

Some two hours before, the Head Constable had entered the house where he had been so constantly and so hospitably entertained, with the firm conviction that Theodore Carden had been the catspaw of a clever, unscrupulous woman; in fact that there had come a repetition, but a hundred times more serious, of that now half-forgotten entanglement which had so nearly brought Carden to grief some seven or eight years before. Once more he had come prepared to do his best to save his friend's son, so far as might be possible, from the consequences of his folly.

But now? Ah, now, the experienced, alert official had to admit to himself that the incidents of the last ten minutes had completely altered his view of the matter. He realised that in any case Theodore Carden was no fool; for the first time that day the terrible suspicion came into Major Lane's mind that the man before him might, after all, be more closely connected with the Jarvice mystery than had seemed possible.

Never, during his long connection with crime, had the Head Constable come across as good an actor, as cool a liar, as he now believed this man of business to be.

Well, he would give Theodore Carden one more chance to tell the truth; Theodore was devoted to his father, so much was certainly true, and perhaps his father would be able to make him understand the gravity of the case. Major Lane felt bitterly sorry that he had come first to the old man—but then, he had so completely believed in the "scrape" theory; and now he hardly knew what to believe!

For the moment, at any rate, so the Head Constable told himself, the mask had fallen; Theodore Carden could not conceal his relief at the other's approaching departure.

"Certainly," he said hastily, "come in this evening by all means; I won't ask you to stay to dinner, for I mean to try and make father go to bed, but later I shall be quite free. If, however, you want to ask me anything about the Jarvice affair, I'm afraid I can't help you much; I've not even read the case with any care."

The old man, still sitting by the fire, had caught a few of the muttered words, and before Major Lane could leave the room Thomas Carden had risen from his chair, his face paler, perhaps, than usual, but once more his collected, dignified self.

"Stay," he said firmly; "having gone so far, I think we should now thresh the matter out."

He walked over to where his son and his friend were standing, and he put his hand on the older man's arm.

"Perhaps I cannot expect you, Lane, to be convinced, as I, of course, have been convinced, by my son's denials. It is, as I told you this afternoon, either a plot on the part of someone who bears a grudge against us, or else—what I think more likely—there are two men in this great town each bearing the name of Theodore Carden. But I appreciate, I deeply appreciate, the generous kindness which made you come and warn us of this impending calamity; but you need not fear that we shall fail to meet it with a complete answer."

"Father! Major Lane! What does this mean?"

For the first time a feeling of misgiving, of sudden fear, swept over Theodore Carden's mind. Without waiting for an answer, he led the way back to the fireplace, and, deliberately drawing forward a chair, motioned to Major Lane to sit down likewise.

"Now then," he said, speaking with considerable authority and decision, "I think I have a right to ask what this is all about! In what way are we, my father and myself, concerned in the Jarvice affair? For my part, Major Lane, I can assure you, and that, if you wish it, on oath, that I did not know Mr. Jarvice, and, to the best of my belief, I have never seen, still less spoken to, Mrs. Jarvice——"

"If that be indeed so," said the man whom he addressed, and who, for the first time, was beginning to feel himself shaken in his belief, nay, in his absolute knowledge, that the young man was perjuring himself, "can you, and will you, explain these letters?" and he drew out of his pocket a folded sheet of foolscap.

Carden bent forward eagerly; there was no doubt, so the Head Constable admitted to himself, as to his eagerness to be brought face to face with the accusation—and yet, at that moment, a strong misgiving came over Major Lane.

Even if Theodore Carden could continue to be the consummate actor he had already proved himself, was it right, was it humane, to subject him to this terrible test, and that, too, before his old father? Whatever the young man's past relation to Mrs. Jarvice, nay, whatever his connection might be with the crime which Major Lane now knew to have been committed, Carden was certainly ignorant of the existence of these terrible, these damnatory documents, and they constituted so far the only proof that Carden had been lying when he denied any knowledge of Mrs. Jarvice. But then, alas! they constituted an irrefutable proof.

With a sudden movement Major Lane withdrew his right hand, that which held the piece of paper.

"Stop a moment, Theodore; do you really wish this discussion to take place before your father? I wonder if you remember"—he paused, and then went on firmly, "an interview you and I had many years ago?"

For the first time the younger man's whole manner changed; a look of fear, of guilt, came over his strong, intelligent face.

"Father," he said imploringly, "I beg you not to listen to Major Lane. He is alluding to a matter which he gave me his word—his word of honour—should never be mentioned to anyone, least of all to you;" then, turning with an angry gesture to the Head Constable, "Was that not so?" he asked imperiously.

"Yes, I admit that by asking you this question I have broken my word, but good God! man, this is no passing scrape that we have to consider now; to-morrow morning all Birmingham will be ringing with your name—with your father's name, Theodore—for by some horrible mischance the papers have got hold of the letters in question. I did my best, but I found I was powerless."

He turned and deliberately looked away, as he added in a low, hesitating voice: "And now, once more I ask you whether we had not better delay this painful discussion until you and I are alone?"

"No!" cried Carden, now thoroughly roused, "certainly not! You have chosen to come and tell my father something about me, and I insist that you tell me here, and at once, what it is of which I am accused."

He instinctively looked at his father for support, and received it in full measure, for at once the old man spoke.

"Yes, Lane, I think my son is right; there's no use in making any more mystery about the matter. I'm sure that the letters you have brought to show Theodore will puzzle him as much as they have me, and that he will be able to assure you that he has no clue either to their contents or to their writer."

Very slowly, with a feeling of genuine grief and shame for the man who seemed incapable of either sorrow or shame, Major Lane held out the folded paper; and then in very pity he looked away as his old friend's son eagerly unrolled the piece of foolscap, placing it close under the lamp-shade in order that he might thoroughly master its contents.

As Theodore Carden completed the trifling action, that of unrolling the piece of paper which was to solve the mystery, he noted, with a curious feeling of relief, that the documents (or were they letters?) regarded by the Head Constable as so damnatory, were but two, the first of some length, the second consisting of a very few lines, and both copied in the fair round hand of Major Lane's confidential clerk.

And then, with no premonitory warning, Carden became the victim of a curious physical illusion.

Staring down at the long piece of blue paper, he found that he was only able to master the signature, in both cases the same, with which each letter terminated. Sometimes only one word, one name—that of *Pansy*—stood out clearly, and then again he seemed only to see the other word, the other name—that of *Jarvice*. The two names appeared to play hide-and-seek with one another, to leap out alternately and smite his eyes, pressing and printing themselves upon his brain.

At last, while he was still staring silently, obstinately, at the black lines dancing before him, he heard the words, and they seemed to be coming from a long way off, "Theodore! Oh, my boy, what is the matter?" and then Major Lane's voice, full of rather angry concern, "Rouse yourself, Carden, you are frightening your father."

"Am I?" he said dully; "I mustn't do that;" then, handing back the sheet of foolscap to the Head Constable, he said hoarsely, "I can't make them out. Will you read them to me?"

> And Major Lane, in passionless accents, read aloud the two letters which he already almost knew by heart.6, LIGHTWOOD PLACE,*January 28th*.
>
> You told me to write to you if ever I was in real trouble and thought you could help me. Oh! Theo, darling, I am in great trouble, and life, especially since that happy time— you know when I mean—is more wretched than ever. You used to say I was extraordinarily pretty, I wonder if you would say so now, for I am simply ill—worn out with worry. He—you know who—has found out something; such a little insignificant thing; and since then he makes my life unbearable with his stupid jealousy. It isn't as if he

> knew about you and me, that would be something real to grumble at, wouldn't it, darling? Sometimes I feel tempted to tell him all about it. How he would stare! He is incapable of understanding anything romantic. However, I'm in no mood for laughing now. He's got a woman in to watch me, a governess, but luckily I've quite got her to be on my side, though of course I haven't told her anything about my private affairs.
>
> Will you meet me one day this week, to-morrow if you can, at No. 15, Calthorpe Street? Four o'clock is the safest time for me. Between the two small shops you will see a swing door with "Madame Paula, Milliner," on it; push it open and go straight upstairs. On the first landing you will see a door with "Gone out, enquire upstairs," on it. Push up the door knob (don't try to turn it) and walk in. The room will be empty, but you will see a door leading to a back room; push *up* the knob and there—there you will find your poor little Pansy, fainting with joy at seeing her big strong Theo again.
>
> Send me a postcard, saying, "Mrs. Jarvice can be fitted on (day you select)." If posted before eleven, it will reach me in time. Of course, I'm running a risk in meeting you *here*, so near my home, but I *must* see you, for I have a great favour to ask you, Theo, and I dare not propose going away even for one day. PANSY JARVICE.

Major Lane paused a moment, then went on:

> Theo, I wrote to you ten days ago, but I have had no answer. I am dreadfully worried; I know you are in Birmingham, for I saw your name in a paper before I wrote to you. I have gone through such terrible days waiting for the postcard I asked you to send me. Write, if only to say you don't want to hear again of poor miserable PANSY JARVICE.

"I suppose you will now admit that you know who wrote these letters?" asked Major Lane sternly.

"Yes—at least I suppose they were written by Mrs. Jarvice."

Theodore Carden spoke with a touch of impatience. The question seemed to him to be, on the part of his father's old friend, a piece of useless cruelty.

"And can you suggest to whom they were written, if not to yourself?"

"No, of course not; I do not doubt that they were written to me," and this time his face was ravaged with a horror and despair to which the other two men had, so far, no clue. "And yet," he added, a touch of surprise in his voice, "I never saw these letters—they never reached me."

"But of course you received others?"

Major Lane spoke with a certain eagerness; then, as the young man seemed to hesitate, he added hastily: "Nay, nay—say nothing that might incriminate yourself."

"But indeed—indeed I have never received a letter from her—that perhaps is why I did not know the handwriting."

"Theodore!" cried his father sharply, "think what you are saying! What you've been shown are only copies—surely you understood that? What Lane has just shown you are copies of letters which purport to have been addressed to you, but which were intercepted on their way to the post—is that not so?" and he turned to the Head Constable.

"Yes," said Major Lane; then he added, very deliberately.

"The originals of these two letters, which were bought for a large sum from Mrs. Jarvice's governess, evidently the woman referred to in the first letter, are now in the hands of the news editor of the *Birmingham Dispatch*. I was shown them as a great favour"—a grim smile distorted, for a moment, the Head Constable's narrow jaw.

"I did my best—for your father's sake, Theodore—to frighten these people into giving them up; I even tried to persuade them to hold them over, but it was no good. I was told that no Birmingham paper had ever had such a—'scoop', I believe, was the word used. You and your father are so well known in this city." And again Theodore Carden marvelled at the cruelty of the man.

Thomas Carden broke in with a touch of impatience:

"But nothing else has been found, my boy! Lane should tell you that the whole theory of your having known Mrs. Jarvice rests on these two letters—which never reached you."

Father and son seemed suddenly to have changed places. The old man spoke in a strong, self-confident tone, but the other, his grey face supported on his hands, was staring fixedly into the fire.

"Yes," said Major Lane, more kindly, "I ought perhaps to tell you that within an hour of my being shown these letters I had Mrs. Jarvice's house once more searched, and nothing was found connecting you with the woman, excepting, I am sorry to say, this;"—and he held out an envelope on which was written in Theodore Carden's clear handwriting the young man's name and business address.

"Now, I should like you to tell me, if you don't mind doing so, where, when, and how this name and address came to be written?"

"Yes, I will certainly tell you."

The young man spoke collectedly; he was beginning to realise the practical outcome of the conversation.

"I wrote that address about the middle of last October, in London, at Mansell's Hotel in Pall Mall East."

"The poor fellow's going to make a clean breast of it at last," so thought Major Lane with a strange feeling of relief, for on the flap of the envelope, which he had kept carefully turned down, was stamped "Mansell's Hotel."

It was in a considerate, almost kindly tone, that the Head Constable next spoke.

"And now, I beg you, for your own sake, to tell me the truth. Perhaps I ought to inform you, before you say anything, that, according to our theory, Mrs. Jarvice was certainly assisted in procuring the drug with which there is no doubt she slowly poisoned her husband. As yet we have no clue as to the person who helped her, but we have ascertained that for the last two months, in fact, from about the date of the first letter addressed to you, a man did purchase minute quantities of this drug at Birmingham, at Wolverhampton, and at Walsall. Now, mind you, I do not suspect, I never have suspected, you of having any hand in that, but I fear you'll have to face the ordeal of being confronted with the various chemists, of whom two declare most positively that they can identify the man who brought them the prescription which obtained him the drug in question."

While Major Lane was speaking, Theodore Carden had to a certain extent regained his self-possession; here, at least, he stood on firm ground.

"Of course, I am prepared to face anything of the kind that may be necessary." He added almost inaudibly: "I have brought it on myself."

Then he turned, his whole voice altering and softening: "Father, perhaps you would not mind my asking Major Lane to go into the library with me? I should prefer to see him alone."

II

And then the days dragged on, a week of days, each containing full measure of bitter and public humiliation; full measure also of feverish suspense, for Theodore Carden did not find it quite so easy as he had thought it would be to clear himself of this serious, and yet preposterous accusation of complicity in murder.

But Major Lane was surprised at the courage and composure with which the young man faced the ordeal of confrontation with the various men, any one of whom, through a simple mistake or nervous lapse of memory, might compel his presence, if not in the dock, then as a witness at the coming murder trial.

At last the awful ordeal was over, for, as a matter of fact, none of those brought face to face with him in the sordid promiscuity of such scenes, singled out Theodore Carden as resembling the mysterious individual who had almost certainly provided Mrs. Jarvice with the means wherewith to poison her husband.

But it was after the need for active defence had passed away that Theodore Carden's true sufferings began.... The moment twilight fell he was haunted, physically and mentally possessed, by the presence of the woman he had known at once so little and so well—that is, of her he now knew to be Pansy Jarvice.

Especially terrible were the solitary evenings of those days when his father was away, performing the task of breaking so much of the truth as could be told to the girl to whom his son had been engaged.

As each afternoon drew in Theodore found himself compelled to remain more or less concealed in the room which overlooked the garden of Waterhead. For, with the approach of night, the suburban road in front of the fine old house was filled by an ever coming and going crowd of bat-like men and women, eager to gaze with morbid curiosity at the dwelling of the man who had undoubtedly been, if not Mrs. Jarvice's accomplice—that, to the annoyance of the sensation-mongers, seemed decidedly open to question—then, her favoured lover.

But to these shameful and grotesque happenings Theodore Carden gave scarce a thought, for it was when he found himself alone in the drawing-room or library that his solitude would become stealthily invaded by an invisible and impalpable wraith.

So disorganised had become his nerves, so pitiable the state of his body and mind, that constantly he seemed conscious of a faint, sweet odour, that of wood violets, a scent closely associated in his thoughts with Pansy Jarvice, with the woman whom he now knew to be a murderess.

He came at last to long for a tangible delusion, for the sight of a bodily shape which he could tell himself was certainly not there. But no such relief was vouchsafed him; and yet once, when sitting in the drawing-room, trying to read a book, he had felt a rounded cheek laid suddenly to his, a curl of silken, scented hair had touched his neck....

Terrifying as was the peopled solitude of his evenings, Carden dreaded their close, for at night, during the whole of each long night, the woman from whom he now felt so awful a repulsion held him prisoner.

From the fleeting doze of utter exhaustion he would be awakened by feeling the pressure of Pansy's soft, slender arms about his neck; they would wind themselves round his shuddering body, enclosing him slowly, inexorably, till he felt as if he must surely die under their gyves-like pressure.

Again—and this, perhaps, was what he learnt to dread in an especial degree—he would be suddenly roused by Pansy's liquid, laughing voice, whispering things of horror in his ear; it was then, and then only, that he found courage to speak, courage to assure her, and so assure himself, that he was in no sense her accomplice, that he had had naught to do with old Jarvice's death. But then there would come answer, in the eager tones he remembered so well, and the awful words found unwilling echo in his heart: "Yes, yes, indeed you helped!"

And now the last day, or rather the last night, had come, for the next morning Theodore Carden was to leave Birmingham, he hoped for ever, for New Zealand.

The few people he had been compelled to see had been strangely kind; quiet and gentle, as folk, no doubt, feel bound to be when in the presence of one condemned. As for Major Lane, he was stretching—no one knew it better than Carden himself—a great point in allowing the young man to leave England before the Jarvice trial.

During those last days, even during those last hours, Theodore deliberately prevented himself from allowing his mind to dwell on his father. He did not know how much the old man had been told, and he had no wish to know. A wall of silence had arisen between the two who had always been so much, nay, in a sense, everything, to one another. Each feared to give way to any emotion, and yet the son knew only too well, and was ashamed of the knowledge, with what relief he would part from his father.

There had been a moment when Major Lane had intimated his belief that the two would go away and make a new life together, but Theodore Carden had put aside the idea with rough decision. Perhaps when he was far away on the other side of the world, the former relations of close love and sympathy, if not of confidence, might be re-established between his father and himself, but this, he felt sure, would never be while they remained face to face.

And now he was lying wide awake in the darkness, in the pretty peaceful room which had once been his nursery, and where he had spent his happy holidays as a schoolboy.

His brain remained abnormally active, but physically he was oppressed by a great weariness; to-night, for the first time, Carden felt the loathsome wraith that haunted him, if not less near, then less malicious, less watchful than usual, above all less eager to assert her power.... Yet, even so, he lay very still, fearing to move lest he should once more feel about his body the clinging, enveloping touch he dreaded with so great a dread.

And then, quite suddenly, there came a strange lightening of his heart. A space of time seemed to have sped by, and Carden, by some mysterious mental process, knew that he was still near home, and not, as would have been natural, in New Zealand. Nay, more, he realised that the unfamiliar place in which he now found himself was Winson Green Gaol, a place which, as a child, he had been taught to think of with fear, fear mingled with a certain sense of mystery and excitement.

Theodore had not thought of the old local prison for years, but now he knew that he and his father were together there, in a small cell lighted by one candle. The wall of silence, raised on both sides by shame and pain, had broken down, but, alas! too late; for, again in some curious inexplicable way, the young man was aware that he lay under sentence of death, and that he was to be hanged early in the morning of which the dawn was only just now breaking.

Yet, strange to say, this knowledge caused him, personally, but little uneasiness, but on his father's account he felt infinitely distressed, and he found himself bending his whole mind to comfort and sustain the old man.

Thus, he heard a voice, which he knew to be his own, saying in an argumentative tone, "I assure you, father, that an extraordinary amount of nonsense is talked nowadays concerning—well, the death penalty. Is it possible that you do not realise that I am escaping a much worse fate—that of having to live on? I wish, dear dad, that I could persuade you of the truth of this."

"If only," muttered the old man in response, "if only, my boy, I could bear it for you;" and Carden saw that his father's face was seared with an awful look of terror and agony.

"But, indeed, father, you do not understand. Believe me, I am not afraid—it will not be so bad after all. So do not—pray, pray, father, do not be so distressed."

And then, with a great start, Theodore Carden awoke—awoke to see the small, spare figure of that same dear father, clothed in the long, old-fashioned linen nightshirt of another day, standing by his bedside.

The old man held a candle in his hand, and was gazing down at his only child with an expression of unutterable woe and grief.

"I will try—I am trying, my boy, not to be unreasonably distressed," he said.

Theodore Carden sat up in bed.

Since this awful thing had come on him, he had never, even for an instant, forgotten self, but now he saw that his sufferings were small compared with those he had brought on the man into whose face he was gazing with red-rimmed, sunken eyes.

For a moment the wild thought came to him that he might try to explain, to justify himself, to prove to his father that in this matter he had but done as others do, and that the punishment was intolerably heavier than the crime; but then, looking up and meeting Thomas Carden's perplexed, questioning eyes, he felt a great rush of shame and horror, not only of himself, but of all those who look at life as he himself had always looked at it; for the first time, he understood the mysterious necessity, as well as the beauty, of abnegation, of renunciation.

"Father," he said, "listen. I will not go away alone; I was mad to think of such a thing. We will go together, you and I,—Lane has told me that such has been your wish,—and then perhaps some day we will come back together."

After this, for the first time for many nights, Theodore Carden fell into a dreamless sleep.

III

A VERY MODERN INSTANCE

Oliver Germaine walked with long, even strides from the Marble Arch to Grosvenor Gate. It was Sunday morning, early in July, and the comparatively deserted portion of the Park which he had chosen was, even so, full of walkers. A good many people, men as well as women, looked at him pleasantly as he went by, for the young man was an attractive, even an arresting personality to the type of person who takes part in Church Parade.

Germaine was tall, slim, dark, so blessed by fate in the mere matter of eyes, nose and mouth, that his looks were often commented on when his wife's beauty was mentioned.

So it was that, as he walked quickly by, a rather vexed expression on his handsome face, almost every man who saw him envied him—if not his looks then his clothes, if not his clothes then his air of being young, healthy, and, to use an ugly modern phrase, in perfect condition.

A nursemaid who watched him pass to and fro several times told herself, rather wistfully, that he was waiting for a loved one, and that the lady, as is the way with loved ones, was late.

The nursemaid was right in one sense, wrong in another. Oliver Germaine was waiting for a lady, but the lady was his married sister. Her name was Fanny Burdon, and her home was in Shropshire. Germaine had a loved one, but she was already his wife, his beautiful, clever Bella, with whom he would so much rather have been now, sitting in their pretty house in West Chapel Street than waiting in the Park for his sister Fanny.

It was really too bad of Fanny to be late! The more so that she would certainly feel aggrieved if, when she did come, her brother made her go straight home with him, instead of taking her down into the crowd of people who were now seething round the Achilles statue. But if Fanny didn't come at once, go home they must, for Bella wouldn't like them to be late—quite a number of people were coming to lunch.

Germaine did not quite know whom, among their crowds of friends, Bella had asked to come in to-day. But certain people, four or five perhaps, would assuredly be there—Mrs. Slade, Bella's great "pal," a nice pretty little woman, with big appealing eyes; also Jenny and Paul Arabin, distant relations of his wife, and once the young couple's only link with the exclusive world of which they now formed so intimate a part.

Then there would be Uvedale.

Germaine's mind dwelt on Uvedale. Bob Uvedale was one of his wife's admirers—in fact Uvedale made no secret of his infatuation for the beautiful Mrs. Germaine, but he was a good fellow, and never made either Bella or himself ridiculous.

Oliver Germaine had remained very simple at heart. He felt sure that Bella could take care of herself; she always behaved with extraordinary prudence and sense,—in fact Oliver was now far less jealous of Bella than he had been in the old days, before she had blossomed into a famous beauty. She was then rather fond of flirting—but her husband had proved the truth of the comfortable old adage concerning safety in numbers. Bella now simply had no time for flirtation! There was no necessity for her to exert herself, she had only to sit still and be admired and adored,—adored, that is, in platonic fashion, admired as you admire a work of art.

Another man who would certainly be lunching with them to-day was Peter Joliffe.

Joliffe was a clever, quaint fellow, whose mission in life was to make people laugh by saying funny things in a serious tone. Joliffe was always fluttering round Bella. He had established himself as a tame cat about the house, and he had, as a matter of fact, been very useful to the young couple, piloting Bella when she was only "the new beauty" amid social quicksands and shallows of which she naturally knew nothing.

Nay, more, Peter Joliffe had introduced the Germaines to some of the very nicest people they knew,—old-fashioned, well-established people, delightful old ladies who called Bella "My pretty dear," courtly old gentlemen who paid her charmingly-turned compliments. Yes, it was nice to think Joliffe would be there to-day; he always helped to make a party go off well.

As for Oliver's sister, Fanny, she would have to sit next Henry Buck. For a brief moment Germaine considered Henry Buck,—Buck who was always called "Rabbit" behind his back, and sometimes to his face.

Germaine hardly knew how it was that they had come to know poor old Rabbit so well. They had met him soon after they were married, and ever since he had stuck to them both with almost pathetic insistence. Oddly enough, he, Oliver, did not reciprocate Henry Buck's feelings of admiring friendship. It was not that he disliked the man, but he had a sort of physical antipathy to him.

The only interesting thing about Henry Buck was his wealth. But then to many people that made him very interesting, for he was really immensely rich, and one of those rather uncommon people, who don't know how to spend their money! Poor Rabbit had been educated at home by a foolish, widowed mother, who had been afraid of letting him play rough games. This was perhaps why he was so dull and awkward—not quite like other people.

Germaine felt rather sorry that Henry Buck would certainly be there to-day. Considering how very little he did for them—no, that was a beastly thing to say, even to oneself!—but considering how very unornamental and uninteresting poor old Rabbit was, it was really very nice of Bella to be so kind to him. She never seemed to mind his being there, and she had even managed to force his company on certain people whose one object in life was to avoid a bore, and who didn't care a button whether a man was a pauper or a millionaire.

Of course Germaine guessed what had happened to Fanny. She had almost certainly gone to hear some fashionable preacher—for Fanny was the sort of woman who likes to cram everything into a visit to London. She was disappointed if every waking hour did not bring with it some new sensation, some new amusement, and this was odd—or so her simple-hearted brother told himself—because all the rest of the year Fanny was content to lead the dull, stodgy life of a small Shropshire squire's wife.

Oliver's irritation increased. It was foolish of Fanny to have come to London just now, in the middle of the season! Hitherto, she and her husband had always come up for a fortnight just before Christmas, and then perhaps again just before Easter. Now she had come up alone, and settled herself into dull lodgings in Marylebone; and then—well, the young man was vaguely aware that Fanny's visit to town was really a scouting expedition. She evidently wanted to see for herself how her brother Oliver and his beautiful wife were "getting on."

Strange to say, Fanny was not quite pleased at Bella's sudden social success—not pleased, and yet quite willing to profit by it. How queer that was! How queer, for the matter of that, most women were! But Bella was not queer—in fact, Bella had been most awfully nice about Fanny, and had never allowed her to suspect, even by as much as a look, that her presence was not welcome. Yet Fanny naturally proved "odd man out" at all those little gatherings to which her lovely sister-in-law made her so carelessly welcome. Fanny knew nothing of the delightful world in which Oliver and Bella now moved; she was quite convinced that she belonged to the very best, exclusive set, and so she did—in Shropshire. But here in town? Why, she was even ignorant of the new social shibboleths; all her notions as to what it was the right thing to do, or to avoid doing, belonged to the year before last!

Take to-day. Fanny would certainly feel cross and disappointed that Bella was not there, in the Park, too; and, as a matter of fact, Germaine had tried to make his wife please his sister in the little matter of Church Parade—but Bella had shaken her head smilingly.

"You know I would do anything for Fanny," she had said, "but really, darling, you mustn't ask me to do *that*—to go into that big, horrid, staring crowd. Why should I? It makes one look so cheap! It would only bore me, and I don't think Fanny would really enjoy having me there," and Bella had smiled a little smile.

Germaine had smiled too,—he really couldn't help it! It was quite true that Fanny would not enjoy seeing Bella looked at, followed,—in a word, triumphing, in the way she did triumph every time she appeared in a place where she was likely to be recognised.

Of course it was odd, when one came to think of it, that Bella, who had been just as pretty two years ago as she was now, should, for some mysterious reason, have been suddenly discovered, by those whose word is law in such matters, to be astonishingly, marvellously beautiful!

An involuntary smile again quivered across Oliver Germaine's good-looking face. He had but little sense of humour, and yet even he saw something almost comic about it—the way that Bella, his darling, pretty little Bella, had suddenly been exalted—hoisted up, as it were, on to a pinnacle. She was now what the Londoners of a hundred years ago would have called "the reigning toast"—so an amusing old fellow, who was a great authority on history, had told him a few days ago.

Still, he ought to make allowances for his sister Fanny. It was not in human nature—or so Oliver believed—for any woman, even for such a good sort as Fanny undoubtedly was, to be really pleased at another woman's triumph.

Small wonder that, to use his sister's favourite expression, Fanny could not make it out! It was unfortunate that Bella's fame—that fame of which the young husband was half ashamed and half proud—had actually penetrated to the dull village where his only sister held high state as wife of the lord of the manor.

Since Fanny had been in town she had said little things to him about Bella's position as reigning beauty—not altogether kindly or nice little things. Even yesterday she had observed, with a touch of sharp criticism in her voice, "I wonder, dear old boy, why you allow Bella's photograph to appear in all those low papers!" and Oliver had shrugged his shoulders, not knowing what to answer, but comfortably sure, in a brotherly way, that Fanny would have been quite willing to see her own fair features reproduced in similar fashion, had it occurred to any of the editors of these same enterprising papers to ask for the loan of her photograph.

As a matter of fact, he had remembered, even while she was speaking, a monstrously ugly photograph of Fanny,—Fanny surrounded by her dogs and children,—which had appeared in a well-known lady's paper. Why, she had actually sent the paper to him, marked! But Oliver magnanimously refrained from reminding her of this,—the more so, that Fanny had hurried on from the trifling question of Bella's portrait to the more serious and unpleasant one of her brother's moderate income.

But, as Germaine now told himself complacently, he had been very short with her. In fact he had administered a good brotherly snub to inquisitive Fanny. She had no business to ask him a lot of questions concerning the way he and Bella chose to spend their income; it was no business of hers how the money was spent. Unfortunately Fanny did consider it her business, simply owing to the fact that she was Oliver's only sister, and very fond of him,—that went without saying,—and that unluckily her husband was Oliver's trustee. So it was that she had shown extraordinary curiosity as to how her brother and his wife managed to live in the way they did, on the income she knew they had.

"Do you know," she had said gravely, "exactly what your income is?" Oliver had nodded impatiently. Of course he knew, roughly speaking, that he and Bella had a little over two thousand a year——

"Two thousand and sixty-one pounds, eighteen shillings," she had gone on impressively. "At least that was what it was last year, for I asked Dick." Now Dick was Fanny's husband, and a most excellent fellow, but hopelessly under Fanny's thumb.

Oliver Germaine had not always been so well off. In fact, when he first met Bella—something like six years ago—he had been a subaltern, with a very small private income, in a Line regiment. And it was on that small income that the loveliest girl in Southsea—now the most beautiful woman in London—had married him. Then had come an immense, unlooked-for piece of good fortune!

A distant Scotch cousin, a crusty old chap, of whom all the Germaines were afraid, and who had constantly declared it to be his intention to leave his money outside his own family, had chosen to make Oliver his heir, and had appointed Fanny's husband, the steady-going, rather dull Shropshire squire, as trustee.

Of course Oliver, and even more Bella, knew now that the fortune which had seemed then to make them rich beyond their wildest dreams, was not so very much after all. But still, at first, it had been plenty—plenty for everything they could reasonably require.

But when Bella had become a famous beauty, they had of course to spend rather more, and about a year ago they had gone through rather a disagreeable moment. The little house in West Chapel Street which had seemed so cheap had proved more expensive than they had expected. However, Dick, as trustee, had stretched a point in his brother-in-law's favour, and the slight shrinkage which had resulted in the Germaines' income mattered not at all from the practical point of view, for the simple reason that they went on spending as much as, in fact rather more than, they had done before—but it was tiresome having to pay, as they now had to do, an insurance premium.

Still, it was too bad of Fanny to have spoken as she had done, for Bella was wonderfully economical. Take one simple matter; all their friends, or at any rate the majority of them, had motors as a matter of course, but Bella, when she was not driving, as she generally did, in a car lent her by some kind acquaintance, contented herself with jobbing an old-fashioned brougham.

This restraint was the more commendable inasmuch that a friend had lately pointed out to her a way in which one could run a motor brougham in town on almost nothing at all. One bought a second-hand car for about seventy-five pounds; it was kept for one at a garage for fifteen shillings a week, and one looked out for a gentleman chauffeur who loved motoring for its own sake, and who had some little means of his own. With care the whole thing need not cost more than a hundred and fifty pounds the first year, and less the second. They could not afford to do this just yet, though Bella was convinced it would be true economy, but Oliver hoped to start something of the kind the following winter.

Of course Oliver was never exactly easy about money. Everything always cost just a little more than he expected. It sounded absurd, and he would not have said so to anyone but himself, but they had to live up to Bella's reputation—that is, they had to go everywhere, and do everything. Yet neither of them lacked proper pride. They differed from some people they knew—that is, they did not (more than they could help) live on their rich friends. Their only real extravagance last year had been sharing a house during Goodwood week. That had let them in for a great deal more than they had expected—in fact, not to put too fine a point on it, they had been rooked, regularly rooked, and by people whom they had thought their intimate friends!

Germaine sighed impatiently. This little uneasiness about money was the one spot on a very bright sun. But he had no wish to confide this fact to Fanny! Fanny would be certain to blame Bella. He remembered very well, though she had apparently forgotten it, the way Fanny had behaved at the time of his marriage.

The fact that the girl he wished so ardently to make his wife was lovely (no one could have denied that even then), and quite sufficiently well connected, had not counterbalanced, from the prudent sister's point of view, Bella Arabin's lack of fortune and her having been brought up in such a "mixed" place (whatever that might mean) as Southsea.

But Bella had never borne malice; and far from being spoilt or rendered "uppish" by her sudden intoxicating success, Bella was, if anything, nicer than before. She and Oliver were still devoted, still happier together than apart; their quarrels, so far, had been only lovers' quarrels....

Germaine grew restless—restless and tired. He had not had such a thinking bout for a long time. Just as he reached Grosvenor Gate for the fifth or sixth time, it struck a quarter-past one. In a sense there was plenty of time, for they lunched at a quarter to two; he would give Fanny ten more minutes and then go off home without her.

The young man looked round. Every bench was full, but there were plenty of empty chairs. He dragged one of them forward, and placed it with its back to a large tree. From there he could see everyone who came in and out of the gate, and so he and Fanny would not lose a moment looking for one another. But, though many went out, very few came in; the Park was beginning to empty.

Suddenly two middle-aged women, the one very stout, the other very thin, walked slowly through the gate. They struck across Germaine's line of vision, and for a moment his dark eyes rested on them indifferently. Then his gaze changed into something like attention, for he had a vague impression of having seen the elder of these two women before. What was more, he felt certain he had seen her in some vaguely unpleasant connection.

For a moment he believed her to be one of the cook-housekeepers with whom he and Bella had grappled during the earlier days of their married life. But no, this short stout woman with the shrewd, powerful face Germaine seemed to know, did not look like a servant. Even he could see that her black clothes were handsome and costly, if rather too warm for a fine July day. Her thin, nervous-looking companion was also dressed with some pretension and research, but she lacked the other's look of stout prosperity.

They were typical Londoners, of the kind to be seen on the route of every Royal procession, and standing among the crowd outside the church door at every fashionable marriage—women who, if they had lived in the London of the Georges, would have walked a good many miles to see a fellow-creature swing. But to Oliver Germaine they were simply a couple of unattractive-looking women, one of whom he thought he had seen before, and whose proximity was faintly disagreeable.

Germaine's mind had dwelt on them longer than it would otherwise have done because, when just in front of him, they stopped short and hesitated; then, looking round them much as Germaine himself had looked round a few minutes before, and, the elder woman taking the lead, each dragged a chair forward, and sat down a yard or so to the young man's right, the trunk of the tree stretching its gnarled grey girth between.

Seven minutes of the ten Oliver meant to allow Fanny had now gone by, and he felt inclined to cut the other three minutes short, and go straight home. After all, it was too bad of her to be so unpunctual!

And then, striking on his ear, shreds of the conversation which was taking place between the two women sitting near him began to penetrate Oliver Germaine's brain. Names fell on his ear—Christian names, surnames, with which he was familiar, evoking the personalities of men and women with whom he was on terms of acquaintance, in some cases of close friendship.

Unconsciously his clasped hands tightened on the knob of his stick, and he caught himself listening—listening with a queer mixture of morbid interest and growing disgust.

It was the elder woman who spoke the most, and she was a good speaker, with that trick,—self-taught, instinctive,—of making the people of whom she was speaking leap up before the listener. Now and again she was interrupted by little shrieks of astonishment and horror—her companion's way of paying tribute to the interesting nature of the conversation.

How on earth—so Oliver Germaine asked himself with heating cheek— had the woman obtained her peculiarly intimate knowledge of those of whom she was speaking? The people, these men and women, especially women, whose lives, the inner cores of whose existences, were being probed and ruthlessly exposed, almost all belonged to the Germaines' own particular set,—if indeed such a prosperous and popular couple as were Oliver and Bella, could be said to have a particular set in that delightful world into which they had only comparatively lately effected an entrance, and of which the strands all intermingle the one with the other.

Germaine was too young, he had been too happy, he was too instinctively kindly, to concern himself with other people's private affairs, save in a wholly impersonal fashion. He had always avoided the hidden, unspoken side of life; when certain secrets were confided to him they dropped quickly out of his mind; ugly gossip passed him by.

Yet now he found himself listening to very ugly gossip; some feeling outside himself, some instinct which for the moment mastered him, made him stay on there, eavesdropping.

For the moment the stream of venom was directed against Mrs. Slade, the pretty, harmless little woman whom he would see within the next hour sitting at his own table. She was one of Bella's special friends, and Oliver had got quite fond of her, the more so that he was well aware that she was in a difficult position, owing to the fact, not of her seeking, or so the Germaines believed, that her husband spent most of his life away from her, abroad.

In this special case, Germaine knew something of the hidden wounds; it was horrible to hear this—this old devil engaged in plucking the scabs from these same wounds, and exposing to her vulgar companion the shifts to which the unfortunate little woman was put. Nay, more, she said certain things concerning Mrs. Slade which, if they were true, or even only half true, made the poor little soul under discussion no fit friend or companion for Germaine's own spotless wife, Bella....

The burden of the old woman's talk was money, how people got money, how they spent money, how they did without money. That was the idea running through all her conversation, although it was, of course, concerned with many uglier things than money.

Had they been men speaking Germaine would have been sufficiently filled with righteous indignation to have found words with which to rebuke, even to threaten them, but they were women, common women, and he felt tongue-tied, helpless.

And then, suddenly, there leapt into the conversation his own name, or rather that of his wife, the woman of whom he felt so exultantly, so selflessly proud. The allusion came in the form of a question, a question spoken in a shrill and odious Cockney accent.

"I should like to see that Mrs. Germaine. I wonder if she ever comes into the Park———"

"Not she! At any rate not on Sunday. Why she'd be mobbed!" snapped out the other.

"You don't say so! Do people run after her as much as that?"

"There's been nothing like it since Mrs. Jersey. I used to see people get up on chairs to see Mrs. Jersey go by. Not that I ever thought much of her figure—great, ugly, square shoulders. She started those square shoulders, and they've never really died out."

"Mrs. Germaine's quite another sort of beauty, the pocket Venus style, isn't she? I suppose you've had a lot to do with making her the rage," said the friend admiringly.

"I don't know about that—her kind of figure dresses itself. She's the sort that gets there anyhow. She's got that 'jennysayquoy' air, as the French put it, that makes folk turn round and stare. She gets her looks from her mother; I remember the mother—her name was Arabin—when I was with Cerise. They weren't London people—they was military. Mrs. Arabin had such pretty coaxing ways, same as the daughter has. Cerise used to let her have the things ever so much cheaper than she charged her other customers, but it paid her too."

Germaine breathed a little more easily. He knew now who this woman was. She was a certain Mrs. Bliss, Bella's dressmaker, in her way a famous old lady, whom Bella's set greatly preferred to the other dressmakers in vogue. It was Mrs. Bliss, so he remembered having heard, who had introduced some years ago the picturesque style of dressing with which his sister Fanny found such fault, and which remains loftily indifferent to the fashion.

Oliver recollected now where and when he had seen her; there had been some little trouble about an item in his wife's bill, and Bella had made him go with her to face the formidable Mrs. Bliss in the old-fashioned house in Sackville Street where the dressmaker wielded her powerful sceptre. That was before Bella had become a fashionable beauty, and Mrs. Bliss had been rather short with them both, unwilling to admit that she was wrong, although the figures proving her so stared her in the face.

And then Germaine remembered other occasions with which Mrs. Bliss's name, though not her personality, were associated. He had made out cheques to her, larger cheques than Bella could manage out of her allowance. But that was some time ago; his wife must now have given up dealing with her; and he felt glad, very glad, that this was so. A woman with such a tongue was a danger to society,—not that anyone need believe a word she said....

Suddenly the shrill Cockney voice asked yet another question concerning the beautiful Mrs. Germaine. It was couched in what the speaker would probably have described as perfectly ladylike and delicate language, but its purport was unmistakable, and Germaine made a restless movement; then he became almost rigidly still—a man cannot turn and strike a woman on the mouth.

"N-o-o, I don't think so." Mrs. Bliss spoke guardedly. "She's a lot of gentlemen buzzing around her, but that's only to be expected; and as far as I can hear there's not one that buzzes closer than another. To tell you the truth, Sophy, I'm puzzled about those Germaines. It's no business of mine, of course, but she spends three times as much as she did when I first began dressing her and she don't mind now what she does pay,—very different to what she used to do! It's only the best that's good enough for my lady now."

"Germaine's an army chap, isn't he?"

"He was—and a handsome fellow he is, too. He came into a good bit of money just after they got married, but that must be melting pretty quick. Why, she goes everywhere! Last season she really wore her clothes out. They"—she waved her hand comprehensively round a vague area comprising Marylebone and Mayfair—"scratched and fought with each other in order to get her."

"Then I suppose you don't bother about your money."

"Yes, I do," said Mrs. Bliss shortly. "I'm not that kind; I don't work for the King of Prussia, as my French tailor used to say."

There was a pause, and then in a rather different voice Mrs. Bliss went on, "I *do* get my money from Mrs. Germaine, but lately,—well, I won't say lately, but for the last eighteen months or so, *she's always paid me in notes*, two, three, sometimes four hundred pounds at a time, always in five-pound notes."

She spoke in a low voice, and yet, to Oliver Germaine, it seemed as if she shouted the words aloud.

The young man got up, and, careless of the lateness of the hour, walked away without looking around towards the Marble Arch; so alone could he be sure that Mrs. Bliss would not see him, and perchance leap to the recollection of who he was.

The words the woman had said so quietly seemed to be reverberating with loud insistence in his ear: "*She's always paid me in notes.*" "*Two, three, sometimes four hundred pounds.*"

What exactly had Mrs. Bliss meant by this statement? What significance had she intended it to carry? There had been a touch of regret in the hard voice, a hesitation in the way she had conveyed the pregnant confidence, which made Oliver heartsick to remember.

But after a time, as Oliver Germaine walked quickly along, uncaring as to which way he was going, almost running in his desire to outstrip his own thoughts, there came a little lightening of his bewildered misery. It was possible, just possible, that Mrs. Bliss was really thinking of some other customer.

Notes? The idea was really absurd to anyone who knew Bella, as he, Oliver, thank God, knew his wife! Why, there was never any loose money in the house, both he and Bella were always running short of petty cash.

Then the young man remembered, with a sudden tightening of the heart, that this had not been the case lately. During the last few months, since they had moved into their new house, Bella had always had money—plenty of sixpences and shillings, half crowns and half sovereigns—at his disposal. Nay more, looking back, he realised that his wife no longer teased him, as she had once perpetually teased him, for supplements, large or small, to her allowance; he had to face the fact that of late Bella's allowance had borne a surprising resemblance to the widow's cruse; it had actually sufficed for all her wants.

But he had been unsuspecting, utterly unsuspecting, and even now he hardly knew what he did suspect.

The horrible things he had heard Mrs. Bliss say about other people acted and reacted on Germaine's imagination. If these things were true, then the world in which he and Bella lived was corrupt and rotten; and, as even Oliver Germaine knew by personal experience, pitch defiles. If Daphne Slade did the things Mrs. Bliss implied she did, Bella must know it,—know it and condone it. Bella was far too clever to be taken in, as he, Oliver, had been taken in, by Mrs. Slade's pretty pathetic manner, and appealing eyes. If Mrs. Slade took money from men, what an example, what a model—— Germaine's mind refused to complete the thought.

Certain of Oliver's and Bella's old acquaintances—people whom they were too kind to drop, but of whom they couldn't see as much now as they had once done, in the days before Bella became a famous beauty—would sometimes hint darkly as to the wickedness of some of the people they knew. Even Fanny had told him bluntly that Bella had got into a very fast set. "Fast" was the word his sister had used, and it had diverted him.

But was it possible that these people, whom he had thought envious and silly—and that Fanny, his rather narrow-minded and old-fashioned sister,— had been right after all? Was it possible that like so many husbands of whom he had heard, for whom he had felt contempt and pity, he had—as regarded his own cherished wife—lived in a fool's paradise?

Germaine now remembered several things that he had known—known and thought forgotten—for they had been completely apart from his own life. He recalled the case of a man in his own regiment who had shot himself three days after his wife's death. It had been publicly given out that the poor fellow had been mad—distraught with grief; but there had been many to mutter that the truth was far other, and that the man had made a shameful discovery among his dead wife's papers....

Concerning any other woman than Bella, Germaine would have admitted, perhaps reluctantly,—but still, if asked the plain question, he would have admitted, that women are damned tricky creatures, and that—well, that you never can tell!

Again, out of the past, there came back to him, with horrid vividness, the memory of a brief episode which at the time had filled him with a kind of pity, even sympathy.

It was at a ball; he was quite a youngster, in fact it was the year after he had joined, and a woman sitting out with him in a conservatory had fallen into intimate talk, as people so often do amid unfamiliar surroundings. There came a moment when she said to him, with burning, unhappy eyes, "People think I'm a good woman, but I'm not." And she had hurried on to make the nature of her sinning quite clear; she had not passion for her excuse—only lack of means and love of luxury. He had been startled, staggered by the unasked-for confidence—and yet he had not thought much the worse of her; now, retrospectively, he judged her with terrible severity.

But *Bella*? The thought of Bella in such company was inconceivable; and yet, deep in Oliver Germaine's heart, there grew from the seed sown by Mrs. Bliss a upas tree which for the moment overshadowed everything. He was torn with anguished jealousy, which made him forget, excepting as affording a proof of what he feared, the sordid, horrible question of the money.

Germaine had already been jealous of Bella, jealous before their marriage, and jealous since, but that feeling had been nothing, *nothing* to that which now held him in its grip.

As a girl, Bella had been a flirt, and, as she had since confessed more than once, she had loved to make Oliver miserable. Then, for some time after their marriage he had been angered at the way she had welcomed and courted admiration. But he had never doubted her, never for a moment thought that her love was leaving him, still less that her flirtations held any really sinister intent. He now remembered how a man, a fool of a fellow, had once brought her a beautiful jewel by way of a Christmas gift; but it had annoyed her, and, without saying anything about it to Oliver at the time, she had actually made the man take back his present!

Was it conceivable that in three or four short years Bella could have entirely altered—have become to all intents and purposes, not only another woman, but a woman of a type,—as even he was well aware, a very common type,—he would not have cared to hear mentioned in her presence?

Germaine was now at the Marble Arch. After a moment's bewildered hesitation, he went up Oxford Street, and then took a turning which would ultimately lead him home; home where Bella must be impatiently awaiting him—home where their intimates had already doubtless gathered together for lunch.

And then, during his walk through the now deserted and sun-baked streets and byways of Mayfair, Oliver Germaine passed in slow review the men and the women who composed his own and Bella's intimate circle. They rose in blurred outline against the background of his memory, and gradually the women fell out, and only the men remained,—two men, for Henry Buck did not count.

Which of these two men who came about his house in the guise of close friends, had planned to steal, to buy, the wife on whose absolute purity and honour he would an hour ago have staked his life?

Germaine's fevered mind leapt on Bob Uvedale. What were Uvedale's relations, his real relations, with Bella? Oliver, so he now told himself sorely, was not quite a fool; he had known men who hid the deepest, tenderest—he would not say the most dishonourable—feelings, towards a married woman, under the skilful pretence of frank laughing flirtation.

Uvedale, when all was said and done, was an adventurer, living on his wits. He talked of his poverty, talked of it over-much, but he often made considerable sums of money; in fact twice, in moments of unwonted expansiveness, Uvedale had offered to put Germaine on to a "good thing," to share with him a tip which had been given him by one of his financial friends. Germaine now remembered, with a sick feeling of anger, how seriously annoyed Bella had been to find that her husband had refused to have anything to do with it; nay more, how she had taunted him afterwards when the "good thing" had turned out good after all. But that was long ago, when they had first known Uvedale.

They now knew Uvedale too well—at least Bella did. Oliver was an outdoor man; he hated crowds. He remembered how often Uvedale took his place as Bella's companion at those semi-public gatherings, charity fêtes, and so on, which apparently amused her, and where the presence of the beautiful Mrs. Germaine was always eagerly desired.

Germaine's mind next glanced with jealous anguished suspicion at another man who was constantly with Bella—Peter Joliffe.

There was a great, almost a ludicrous, contrast between Uvedale and Joliffe. Uvedale, so Germaine dimly realised even now, was a man with a wider, more generous, outlook on life than the other, capable of deeper depths, of higher heights.

Joliffe was well off; and, as the Germaines had been told very early in their acquaintance with him, he had the reputation of being "near." But Bella and Oliver had both agreed that this was not true. Only the other day Bella had spoken very warmly of Joliffe; when they had moved into their new house he had given them a Sheraton bureau, a very charming and certainly by no means a cheap piece of old furniture. Oliver had supposed it to be a delicate way of paying back some of their constant hospitality, for Joliffe was perpetually with Bella.

Time after time Germaine had come in and found Joliffe sitting with her; walking through the hall he had heard her peals of laughter at Joliffe's witticisms, the funny things he said with his serious face.

But after all jesters are men of like passions to their melancholy brethren; they can, and do, throw off the grinning mask. Bella had said, only yesterday, "There's more in Peter than you think, Oliver. Believe me, there is!" Bella always called Joliffe Peter,—she was more formal with Bob Uvedale.

Germaine now reminded himself that Joliffe did not like Uvedale, and that Uvedale did not like Joliffe. There seemed a deep, unspoken antagonism between the two men, who were yet so constantly meeting. Joliffe had gone so far as to say something—not exactly disagreeable, but condemnatory—of Uvedale's city connections, to Germaine. Joliffe was annoyed, distinctly annoyed at the way Bella went about with Uvedale, and by the fact that she often introduced him to people whose acquaintance she had herself made through Joliffe.

What had he, Oliver Germaine, been about, to allow his wife to become so intimate with two men, of whom he knew nothing? Yesterday he would have said Uvedale and Joliffe were his closest pals. But what did he really know of either of them—of their secret thoughts—their deep desires and ambitions—their shames and secret sins? Nothing—nothing. Bella's husband knew as little of Uvedale and Joliffe—in fact, till to-day, far less than they knew of him, for one or the other of these men was his enemy, and had betrayed, very basely, his hospitality.

Germaine had now lashed himself into the certainty that he was that most miserable and pitiable of civilised beings, the trusting, kindly, nay more, adoring husband, whose wife betrays him with his friend.

When others had laughed, as men have laughed, and will ever laugh, at similar ironic juxtapositions of fate, Germaine had remained grave, for he had a sensitive heart—a heart which made him realise something of what lay beneath such tales. Now he told himself that so no doubt he himself was being laughed at by the many, pitied—the thought stung deeper—by the few.

As he at last turned into Curzon Street, and so was within a few yards of his house, it struck two o'clock. By now they must all be waiting for him, and Bella would be angry, as angry as she ever allowed her sweet-tempered nature to be. But Germaine told himself savagely that he didn't care,—he was sorry to be so near home, to know that in a few moments he would have to command himself, to pretend light-hearted indifference before a crowd of people most of whom he now feared—ay, feared and hated, for they must all have long suspected what he only now knew to be the truth.

Some one touched him. He started violently. It was his sister, Fanny, pouring out a confused stream of apologies and explanations. He stared at her in silence, and she thought he was so seriously annoyed, so "put out" that he could not trust himself to speak.

But though, as they stood there face to face, he dimly realised what his sister was trying to say, how she was trying to explain her failure to keep her appointment with him in the Park, Germaine could not have told, had his life depended on it, the nature of her excuse.

Together they walked side by side to the door of his house, and, as he rang the bell, as he knocked, he remembered with a pang of jealous anguish that Bella had asked him, when they moved into this house, not to use a latch-key in the daytime; she had explained to him that to do so prevented the servants keeping up to the mark, and he had obeyed her, as he always did obey her. This trifle made his anger, for the moment his impotent anger, become colder, clarified.

It was only an hour later, but at last they were all gone, these people whom Oliver Germaine had now begun to hate and suspect, each in their different measure, women and men. Everyone had left, that is, excepting Henry Buck and Fanny; and Fanny was just going away, Oliver seeing her off at the front door.

Germaine believed that he had carried himself well. True, Uvedale had said to him, "Feeling a bit chippy, old chap?" and twice he had noticed Joliffe's rather cold grey eyes fixed attentively on his face, but under the chatter of the women—Jenny Arabin was a great talker and in a harmless sort of way a great gossip, always knowing everybody's business better than they did themselves—under cover of the women's chatter, he had been able to remain silent, and, whatever the two men present had suspected,—one of the two forced thereto by his own conscience,—Bella had certainly noticed nothing. She had not even seen, as his sister had seen, that Oliver looked tired and unlike himself.

Why, just now Fanny had spoken to him solicitously about his health—blundering, tactless, Fanny had actually asked him if anything special were worrying him!

He shut the door on his sister, and crossed the little hall. The time had now come when he must have it out with Bella.

Then, suddenly, there came over Germaine a feeling as if he had been living through a hideous nightmare. If that were indeed so, then his whole life would not be too long to secretly atone to Bella for his horrible suspicion.

It seemed suddenly monstrous that he should suspect Bella on the word of a Mrs. Bliss. His wife had a right, after all, to pay her dressmaker in banknotes if the fancy seized her. Sometimes when Bella did something that he, Oliver, did not like or approve, she explained that her mother had done the same thing, and the excuse always irritated him, left him without an answer.

Supposing that Bella were now to tell him that the late Mrs. Arabin, whose reputation for a certain daring liveliness and exceeding beauty still lingered in the ever-shifting naval and military society where he had first met his wife, always paid her bills in notes and cash rather than by cheque—what then?

He walked up the staircase; Henry Buck passed him coming down. Germaine's eyes rested on the awkward figure, the plain, good-natured face. Rabbit was certainly lacking in tact; he always outstayed all their other guests, and he never knew when Bella was tired, but still he was the one human being present at the little lunch party at whom Oliver had been able to look without a feeling of unease.

Slowly he turned the painted china knob of the drawing-room door.

Bella was standing before the Sheraton bureau which had been the gift of Peter Joliffe. She had apparently been putting something away; Germaine heard the click of the lock. She turned round quickly, and her husband thought there was a look of constraint on her face.

"Why, Oliver," she said, "I thought you were going out with Fanny this afternoon!"

"With Fanny?" he stammered, "I never thought of doing such a thing."

"But you're not going to stay in, are you?"

He looked at her attentively, and again there surged up in his heart wild jealousy and suspicion. Why did she ask whether he was going to stay in? Which of the two men who had just left the house was she expecting to come back as soon as he, poor deluded fool, was safely out of the way?

But Bella went on speaking rather quickly: "I shan't go out. I'm tired. Besides, I'm expecting some people to tea. So perhaps I'd better go and take my hat off. I shall only be a few minutes; do wait till I come back." Bella spoke rather breathlessly, moving across the room towards the door.

Then she didn't want him to go out? He had wronged her in this, at any rate. Germaine stared at the door through which his wife had just gone with a feeling of miserable uncertainty.

Then his eye travelled round to the place where she had been standing just now, in front of Joliffe's bureau. A glance at Bella's bank-book would set his mind at rest one way or the other. It would go far to prove or disprove the story Mrs. Bliss had told, for it would show if Bella were indeed in the habit of drawing considerable cheques to "self." Why hadn't he thought of this simple test before,—before shaming himself and shaming his wife by base suspicions?

And yet Oliver, for some few moments, stood in the middle of the room irresolute. Yesterday it would never have occurred to him that Bella would mind his looking at her bank-book, although, as a matter of fact he never had looked at it. She was a tidy little woman; he knew that everything under the flap which he had seen her close down so quickly just now would be exquisitely neat; he knew the exact spot where her bank-book was to be found.

With a curious feeling that he was doing something dishonourable,—and it was a feeling which sat very uneasily on Oliver Germaine,—he took hold of the little brass knob and slid up the flap of the sloping desk.

The bank-book closed the ranks of the red household books over which in old days, when they were first married, before he had come into his fortune, he had actually seen Bella shed tears.

With fingers that felt numb he took up the little vellum-bound book and opened it at the page containing the latest items.

There, on the credit side, was the sum of money which had been paid in, to his bankers' order, on the last quarter day. On the debit side were a few cheques made out to trades-people. There was not a single cheque made out to "self" on the page at which he was looking; but—but of course it was possible that Bella, like so many women, added a few pounds for change every time she settled a tradesman's account.

He turned several leaves of the little book backwards——Here was a page which bore the date of three years ago; and here, as he had feared to find, there were constant, small entries to "self"....

By the empty place on the shelf where the bank-book had stood was a gilt file for bills, a pretty little toy which had been given her, so the husband now remembered, by Uvedale. The letters composing the word "paid" were twisted round the handle—horrible symbolic word!

He took up the file and ran his fingers through the receipted bills.

Ah! here at last, was one which bore the name of Mrs. Bliss.

The amount of the bill amazed him,—eight hundred and seventy-one pounds, sixteen shillings,—and Bella had paid four hundred pounds on account about a fortnight before. It was the only bill on the file on which there still remained a balance owing. Germaine did not need to look again at his wife's bank-book to see that the majority of the receipted bills had not been paid by cheque.

These bills, so he now became aware with a frightful contraction of the heart, were for all sorts of things—expensive trifles, costly hot-house flowers, extravagantly expensive fruit—which he had enjoyed, and of which he had partaken, believing, if he thought of the matter at all—fool that he had been—that they were being paid for out of his modest income, the income which had once seemed so limitless.

"What are you doing, Oliver? You've no business to look at my things. I never look at yours." He had not heard the door open, and Bella had crept up swiftly behind him; there was some anger, but there was far more fear, in her soft voice.

Germaine turned round and looked at his wife.

Bella had changed her dress, and she was now wearing a painted muslin gown, her slender waist girdled with a blue ribbon. She looked exquisitely lovely, and so young,—a girl, a young and innocent girl.

There fell a heavy hand on her rounded shoulder.

"Oliver!" she cried, "you're hurting me!"

He withdrew his hand—quickly.

"Bella," he said, "I only want to ask you one question—I know everything,"—and in answer to a strange look that came over her face he added hurriedly, "Never mind how I found out. I *have* found out, and now I only want to ask you one thing—I—I have a right to know who it is."

"Who it is?" she repeated. "I don't understand what you mean, Oliver? Who—what?" but as Bella Germaine asked the useless question she shrank back; for the first time in their joint lives she felt afraid of Oliver,—afraid, and intensely sorry for him.

A sob rose to her throat. What a shame it was! How on earth could he have found out? She had thought he would go on not knowing—for ever. That this should happen now, when she was so happy too,—when everything was so—so comfortable.

"Tell me—tell me at once, Bella," he said again, shaken almost out of his self-control by her pretended lack of understanding.

But Bella made no answer; she was retreating warily towards the open window; Oliver, poor angry Oliver, could not say much, he could not *do* anything, out on the balcony.

But he grasped her arm. "Come back," he said, "right into the room," and forced her, trembling, down into a low chair. "Now tell me," he repeated. "Don't keep me waiting—I can't stand it. I won't hurt you." He leant over her, grasping her soft arm.

But still Bella said nothing. Her free hand was toying with the fringe of her blue sash. She had become very pale, a sickly yellow colour which made her violet eyes seem blue,—for one terrible moment Oliver thought she was going to faint.

"Why should I tell you?" she muttered at last, "you can't force me to tell you. It's a matter personal to myself. It's no business of yours. I've never spent any of the money on you,"—she unfortunately added, "at least hardly any."

Germaine took his hand from her arm. "My God!" he said, "my God!"

Did a dim gleam of what he was feeling penetrate Bella's brain?

"I don't know why you should trouble to ask me," she said defiantly. "Surely you must know well enough."

"I daresay I'm stupid, but I find it very difficult to guess which of the two, Joliffe or—or Uvedale, is your lover."

"My lover? Joliffe—Uvedale?" Bella started to her feet, the colour rushed back into her face. She was shaking with anger and indignation.

"How dare you insult me so?" she gasped. "You wouldn't have dared to say such a thing if my father had been alive! How dare you say, how dare you *think*, I have a lover?" and then with quivering pain she gave a little cry, "Oh, Oliver!"

Germaine looked at her grimly enough. What a fool—what an abject fool he had been! It fed his anger to see that Bella had so poor an opinion of his intelligence as to suppose that he would believe her denial.

"I know you are lying," he said briefly. "I *know* it is either Joliffe or Uvedale."

"But, Oliver—indeed it isn't!"

She was looking at him with a very curious expression; the fear, the real terror, there had been in her face, had left it. She was staring at her husband as if she were seeking to find on his face some indication of a distraught, unhinged mind.

But he looked cool, collected, stern,—and anger again surged up in Bella's heart. If he were sane she would never—never forgive him his vile suspicion of her. Was it for this that she, Bella, had always gone so straight—never even been tempted to go otherwise, in spite of all the admiration lavished on her?

There had been a time in Bella Germaine's life, some two years before, when she had often rehearsed this scene, when she had been so haunted by the fear of it that it had been a constant nightmare.

But never had she imagined the conversation between Oliver and herself taking the turn it now had. Never, in her most anguished dreams, had Oliver accused her of having—a lover. But she had known, only too well, with what anger and amazement he would learn the lesser truth.

"Peter Joliffe?" she said, with a certain scorn. "How little you know Peter, Oliver, if you think he would be any married woman's lover, let alone mine! Why, Peter's a regular old maid!" She laughed a little hysterically at her simile, and, to her husband, the merriment, which he felt to be genuine, lowered the discussion to a level which was hateful—sordid.

"Then it's Uvedale," he said, heavily; and this time, so he was quick to notice, Bella did not take the trouble to utter a direct denial.

"Bob Uvedale? Are you quite mad? Bob Uvedale is really fond of you, Oliver,—do you honestly think he would make love to me?"

She was actually arguing with him; he shrugged his shoulders with a hopeless gesture.

Then Bella Germaine came quite close up to her husband. She looked at him straight in the eyes.

"I'll tell you," she said. "I see you really don't know. It's—it's——" she hesitated, again a look of shame,—more, of fear,—came into her face, "The person who has been giving me money, Oliver, is Rabbit."

"Rabbit? I don't believe you!"

"You don't believe me?"

Bella drew a long breath. The worst, from her point of view, was now over. She had told the truth,—and Oliver had brushed the truth aside, so possessed by insane jealousy of Peter Joliffe and Bob Uvedale, that he had apparently no room in his heart for anything else.

Bella gave a little sigh of relief. Perhaps, after all, she had made a mistake in being so frightened; men are so queer—perhaps Oliver would feel, as she had now felt for so long, that poor old Rabbit could not find a better use for his money than in making her happy.

She walked over to her pretty desk, and frowned a little as she saw its condition of disarray; the receipted bills which she had found her husband looking over were scattered, even the tradesmen's books had not been put back in their place on the little shelf.

She touched the spring of a rather obvious secret drawer. There had been a time when Bella Germaine had hidden very carefully what she was now about to show Oliver as the certain, triumphant proof that his revolting suspicions were false. But of late she had grown careless.

"If you don't believe me," she said coldly, "look at this, Oliver. I think it will convince you that I told the truth just now."

Bella knew she had a right to be bitterly indignant at her husband's preposterous accusation. But she told herself that now was not the time to show it; she would punish Oliver later on.

She waited a moment and then cried, "Catch!"

Oliver instinctively held out his hands. A bulky envelope fell into them. It was addressed in a handwriting he knew well,—the unformed, and yet meticulous handwriting of Henry Buck. On it was written:

"Mrs. Oliver Germaine,"19, West Chapel Street,"Mayfair."

In the corner were added the words:

"Any one finding this, and taking it to the above address, will be handsomely rewarded."

"Open it!" she said imperiously. "Open it, and see what is inside,—he only brought it to-day."

Oliver opened the envelope. Folded in two pieces of paper was a packet of bank-notes held together with an elastic band.

Germaine looked up questioningly at his wife.

Bella hung her head. She had the grace to feel embarrassed, ashamed in this moment that she believed to be the moment of her exculpation. Her pretty little hands, laden with rings, each one of which had been given her by her husband, were again toying with the fringe of her blue sash.

The silence grew intolerable.

"I know I've been a beast,"—her voice faltered, broke into tears. "I knew you wouldn't like it, but—but you know, Oliver, Rabbit isn't like an ordinary man."

"When did he begin to give you money?" asked Oliver, in a low voice.

"A long time ago," she answered, vaguely.

"He came in one day when I was awfully upset about a bill—a bill of that old devil, Bliss,—and he was so kind, Oliver. He explained how awfully fond he was of us both. He said we were his only friends—I always *have* been nice to him, you know. He said he couldn't spend the money he'd got——"

"How much have you had from him?"

"I can tell you exactly," she said eagerly, and again she moved towards her bureau.

Bella felt utterly dejected; somehow she had not expected Oliver to take the news quite in this way; he looked dreadful—not relieved, as she had thought he would do.

It was with slow lagging steps that she walked back to where her husband was still standing with the envelope and its contents crushed in his right hand.

Bella's love of tidiness and method had stood her in fatally good stead. She had put down all the sums she had received from Henry Buck, but in such a fashion that any one else looking at the figures would not have known money was in question.

Oliver stared down at the piece of paper. Insensibly he straightened his shoulders as if to meet calmly a physical blow. "Are these pounds?" he asked.

She nodded.

"But Bella, it's an enormous sum,—over four thousand."

"I suppose it is," she said listlessly.

Her husband put the paper in his breast pocket; then he hesitated a moment, and Bella thought he was perhaps going to hand her back the envelope and its contents. But that also, to her chagrin, disappeared into his pocket.

"I suppose the money Buck brought you to-day is included in this amount?"

Bella shook her head sadly. "I hadn't time to put it down," she said.

"Well, I'll see what can be done."

"I suppose you mean to pay it all back? I suppose"—her voice was trembling with self-pity—"that we shall have to go and live in the country now?"

He said nothing,—only looked at her with that same cold look of surprise and alienation.

He was leaving the room when a cry from her brought him back. She clutched his hand.

"You've never said you're sorry for the horrible thing you said to me——" and, as he looked at her, still silent, "Oliver! you surely don't think that Rabbit——Why, he's never even squeezed my hand!"

"Stop!" he cried roughly. "Don't be silly, Bella. Of course I don't think anything of the kind. I accept absolutely what you tell me of your relations with Henry Buck."

"Why, there have been no relations with Henry Buck and me," she cried, protesting. "What a hateful word to use, Oliver!"

But he was already out of the door, making his way to the only human being in whom he still felt complete confidence, who, he knew, loved him, in the good old homely sense of the word.

"My dear boy, what *is* the matter?"

Fanny sat up. She had been lying down on the sofa in the sitting-room of her lodgings. Oliver had explained to the servant that he was Mrs. Burdon's brother, and he had been allowed to make his own way up to the drawing-room floor.

"There's a good deal the matter," he said. "The fact is I've made a fool of myself, Fanny,—and I've come to you for help."

Fanny looked up at him, and what she saw checked the words on her lips. She was wide awake now, but rather painfully conscious that she looked untidy. Her smart voile gown—voile was the "smart" material that season—was crumpled. And Oliver's wife, Bella, was always so dreadfully, so unnaturally, tidy and neat,—it was one of the things that perhaps made people think her so much prettier than she really was.

"Of course I will help you," she answered briskly. "Tell me all about it."

"Have you still that five thousand pounds Cousin Andrew left you?"

"Why of course I have,—and it's rather more now, for luckily we didn't put it into Consols; we put it into a Canadian security."

"Is it invested in Dick's name?"

Dick's wife laughed. "No, of course it isn't," she said. "Why should it be?"

"Could you get at it without Dick's knowing?"

"Yes, I suppose I could." There was a touch of wonder in her voice.

"Fanny, I want you to lend me four thousand pounds." Oliver spoke huskily. He was staring out of the window.

His sister looked at him rather queerly for a moment: "Yes, of course I will," she said. And, as he turned to her, his face working,—"You needn't make a fuss about it, dear old boy. You'll pay me back all right, I know that."

"I'll insure against it, and I'll pay you proper interest for it—whatever you're getting now," he said. "And we'll get a lawyer to see that it's all made safe."

"That'll be all right," said Fanny, and then again she gave him that curious, considering look.

Germaine pulled himself together. "You'll think I've been a fool," he exclaimed abruptly,—he had to say something in answer to that look,— "and so I have. But you know—at least you don't know, luckily for you— what it's like to be mixed up with a lot of fellows who are all richer than one is oneself;" and then in a very different tone, one in which his sister felt the ring of truth, "Are you sure Dick won't know, Fanny? I don't want Dick to know."

"Of course he won't know," Fanny smiled. "You don't suppose I tell Dick everything?"

Oliver stared at his sister. He was rather shocked by her admission; till to-day he had thought that all husbands and wives who loved one another told each other everything; and yet, here was Fanny, who hadn't a thought in the world beyond Dick, the children, the dogs—and, and, yes, her brother——

"It's none of Dick's business what I choose to do with my own money—not that he'd mind."

"I think of spreading the re-payment over five years."

"That would be rather too soon," she said; and added, looking away as she spoke, "I don't think it would be fair to Bella."

Oliver reddened, a man's dusky unbecoming blush.

"Bella's been good about it," he said briefly. "She said herself that we should have to go and live in the country. Still, let's make it seven years. I say, Fanny, you *are* a brick," and sitting down by the table, Oliver Germaine broke into hard, painful sobs.

Fanny got up off the sofa. She felt rather shy.

"Don't be so worried," she said. "Bella's a very good sort, and awfully fond of you, old boy. She'll like the country better than you think. Her looks will last twice as long there, and, and—if I were you, Oliver—you and Bella I mean," Fanny got rather mixed, and very red—"well, I'd try and have a baby. Bella would look awfully sweet with a baby. And a baby's no trouble in the country—less trouble than a puppy!"

"Yes, that's true," he said, raising his head, and feeling vaguely comforted. His sister Fanny had a lot of sense. Oliver had always known that.

IV

ACCORDING TO MEREDITH

"Certainly, however, one day these present conditions of marriage will be changed. Marriage will be allowed for a certain period, say ten years."—Mr. GEORGE MEREDITH in the *Daily Mail* of September 24th, 1904.

"Give you some heads? My dear fellow, there need be no question of heads! This is to be a model will. You need simply put down, in as few words as are legally permissible—I know nothing of such things—that I leave all of which I die possessed to my wife."

Philip Dering threw his head back, and gave the man to whom he was speaking, and opposite to whom he was standing, a confident smiling glance. Then he turned and walked quickly over to the narrow, old-fashioned, balconied window which, commanding the wide wind-blown expanse of Abingdon Street, exactly faced the great cavity formed by the arch of the Victoria Tower.

To the right lay the riverside garden, a bright patch of delicate spring colouring and green verdure, bounded by the slow-moving grey waters of the Thames; and Dering's eager eyes travelled on till he saw, detaching itself against an April afternoon horizon, the irregular mass of building formed by Lambeth Palace and the Lollards' Tower.

"I say," he exclaimed, rather suddenly, "this is better than Bedford Park, eh? I suppose a floor in one of these houses would cost us a tremendous lot; even beyond *our* means, Wingfield?" and again a happy smile came over the tense, clear-cut face, still full of youthful glow and enthusiasm.

"You wish everything to go to Louise? All right, I'll make a note of that."

The speaker, a round-faced, slightly bald, shrewd-looking lawyer, took no notice of the, to him, absurd question concerning the rent of floors in Abingdon Street. Still, he looked indulgently at his friend, as he added:

"But wait a bit,—I promise that yours shall be a model will,—only you seem to have forgotten, my dear fellow, that you may out-live your wife. Now, should you have the misfortune to lose Louise, to whom would you wish to devise this fifteen thousand pounds? It's possible, too, though not very probable, I admit, that you may both die at the same time—both be killed in a railway accident for instance."

"Such good fortune may befall us——" Dering spoke quite simply, and accepted the other's short laugh with great good-humour. "Oh! you know what I mean; I always *have* thought husbands and wives—who care, I mean—ought to die on the same day. That they don't do so is one of the many strange mysteries which complicate life. But I say, Wingfield——"

The speaker had turned away from the window. He had again taken up his stand opposite the other's broad writing table, and not even the cheap, ill-made clothes could hide the graceful lines of the tall, active figure, not even the turned-down collar and orange silk tie could destroy the young man's look of rather subtle distinction.

"Failing Louise, I should like this money, at my death, to be divided equally between the young Hintons and your kids," and as the other made a gesture of protest, Dering added quickly:

"What better could I do? Louise is devoted to Jack Hinton's children, and I've always regarded you—I have indeed, old man,—as my one real friend. Of course it's possible now,"—an awkward shy break came into his voice—"it's possible now, I say, that we may have children of our own; I don't suppose you've ever realised how poor, how horribly poor, we've been all these years."

He looked away, avoiding the other man's eyes; then, picking up his hat and stick with a quick, nervous gesture, was gone.

After the door had shut on his friend, Wingfield went on still standing for awhile. His hands mechanically sorted the papers and letters lying on his table into neat little heaps, but his thoughts were travelling backward, through his and Dering's past lives.

The friends had first met at the City of London school, for they were much of an age, though the lawyer looked the elder of the two. Then Dering had gone to Cambridge, and Wingfield, more humbly, to take up life as an articled clerk to a good firm of old-established attorneys. Again, later, they had come together once more, sharing a modest lodging, while Dering earned a small uncertain income by contributing to the literary weeklies, by "ghosting" writers more fortunate than himself, by tutoring whenever he got the chance,—in a word, by resorting to the few expedients open to the honest educated Londoner lacking a definite profession.

The two men had not parted company till Dering, enabled to do so with the help of a small legacy, had chosen to marry a Danish girl, as good-looking, as high-minded, as unpractical as himself.

But stay, had Louise Dering proved herself so unpractical during the early years of her married life?

Wingfield, standing there, his mind steeped in memories, compared her, with an unconscious critical sigh, with his own stolid, unimaginative wife, Kate. As he did so he wondered whether, after all, Dering had not known how to make the best of both worlds; and yet he and his Louise had gone through some bad times together.

Wingfield had been the one intimate of the young couple when they began their married life in a three-roomed flat in Gray's Inn; and he had been aware, painfully so, of the incessant watchful struggle with money difficulties, never mentioned while the struggle was in being, for only the rich can afford to complain of poverty. He had admired, it might almost be said he had reverenced with all his heart, the high courage then shown by his friend's wife.

During those first difficult years, when he, Wingfield, could do nothing for them, Louise had gone without the help of even the least adequate servant. The women of her nation are taught housewifery as an indispensable feminine accomplishment, and so she had scrubbed and sung, cooked and read, made and mended, for Philip and herself.

Wingfield was glad to remember that it was he who had at last found Dering regular employment; he who had so far thrown prudence aside as to persuade one of his first and most valuable clients to appoint his clever if eccentric friend secretary to a company formed to exploit a new invention. The work had proved congenial; Dering had done admirably well, and now, when his salary had just been raised to four hundred a year, a distant, almost unknown, cousin of his dead mother's had left him fifteen thousand pounds!

At last James Wingfield sat down. He began making notes of the instructions he had just received, though as he did so he knew well enough that he could not bring himself to draw up a will by which his own children might so greatly benefit.

Then, as he sat, pen in hand, wondering with a certain discomfort as to what ought to be the practical effect of the conversation, there suddenly came a sound of hurrying feet up the shallow oak staircase, and through the door, flung open quickly and unceremoniously, strode once more Philip Dering.

"I say, I've forgotten something!" he exclaimed, and then, as Wingfield instinctively looked round the bare spacious room—"No, I didn't leave anything behind me. I simply forgot to ask you one very important question——"

He took off his hat, put it down with a certain deliberation, then drew up a chair, and placed himself astride on it, an action which to the other suddenly seemed to blot out the years which had gone by since they had been housemates together.

"As I went down your jolly old staircase, Wingfield, it suddenly occurred to me that making a will may not be quite so simple a matter as I once thought it——"

He hesitated a moment, then went on:—"So I've come back to ask you the meaning of the term 'proving a will.' What I really want to get at, old man, is whether my wife, if she became a widow, would have to give any actual legal proof of our marriage? Would she be compelled, I mean, to show her 'marriage lines'?"

Wingfield hesitated. The question took him by surprise.

"I fancy that would depend," he said, "on the actual wording of the will, but all that sort of thing is a mere formality, and of course any solicitor employed by her would see to it. By the way, I suppose you were married in Denmark?" He frowned, annoyed with himself for having forgotten a fact with which he must have been once well acquainted. "If you had asked me to be your best man," he added with a vexed laugh, "I shouldn't have forgotten the circumstances."

Dering tipped the chair which he was bestriding a little nearer to the edge of the table which stood between himself and Wingfield; a curious look, a look half humorous, half deprecating, but in no sense ashamed, came over his sensitive, mobile face.

"No," he said, at length, "we were not married in Denmark. Neither were we married in England. In fact, there was no ceremony at all."

The eyes of the two men, of the speaker and of his listener, met for a moment; but Wingfield, to the other's sudden uneasy surprise, made no comment on what he had just heard.

Dering sprang up, and during the rest of their talk he walked, with short, quick strides, from the door to the window, from the window to the door.

"I wanted to tell you at the time, but Louise would not have it; though I told her that in principle—not, of course, in practice—you thoroughly agreed with me—I mean with us. Nay, more, that you, with your clear, legal mind, had always realised, even more than I could do, the utter absurdity of making such a contract as that of marriage—which of all contracts is the most intimately personal, and which least affects the interests of those outside the contracting parties—the only legal contract which can't be rescinded or dissolved by mutual agreement! Then again, you must admit that there was one really good reason why we should not tell you the truth; you already liked Kate, and Louise, don't you remember, used to play chaperon. Now, Kate's people, you know——!"

All the humour had gone out of Dering's face, but the deprecating look had deepened.

The lawyer made a strong effort over himself. He had felt for a moment keenly hurt, and not a little angry.

"I don't think," he said quietly, "that there is any need of explanations or apologies between us. Of course, I can't help feeling very much surprised, and that in spite of our old theoretical talks and discussions, concerning—well, this subject. But I don't doubt that in the circumstances you did quite right. Mind you, I don't mean about the marriage," he quickly corrected himself, "but only as to the concealment from me."

He waited a moment, and then went on, hesitatingly: "But even now I don't really understand what happened—I should like to know a little more——"

Dering stayed his walk across the room, and stood opposite his friend. He felt a great wish to justify himself, and to win Wingfield's retrospective sympathy.

"I will tell you everything there is to tell!" he cried eagerly; "indeed, it can all be told in a moment. My wife and I entered into a personal contract together, which we arranged, provisionally, of course, should last ten years. Louise was quite willing, absolutely willing...." For the first time there came a defensive note in the eager voice. "You see the idea—that of leasehold marriage? We used to talk about it, you and I, of course only as a Utopian possibility. All I can say is that I had the good fortune to meet with a woman with whom I was able to try the experiment; and all I can tell you is—well, I need not tell *you*, Wingfield, that there has never been a happier marriage than ours." Again Dering started pacing up and down the room. "Louise has been everything—everything—everything—that such a man as myself could have looked for in a wife!"

"And has no one ever guessed—has no one ever known?" asked the other, rather sternly.

"Absolutely no one! Yes, wait a moment—there has been one exception. Louise told Gerda Hinton. You know they became very intimate after we went to Bedford Park, and Louise thought Gerda ought to know. But it made no difference—no difference at all!" he added, emphatically; "for in fact poor Gerda practically left her baby to Louise's care."

"And that worthless creature, Jack Hinton—does he know too?"

"No, I don't think so; in fact I may say most decidedly not—but of course Gerda may have told him, though for my part I don't believe that husbands and wives share their friends' secrets. Still, you are quite at liberty to tell Kate."

"No," said Wingfield, "I don't intend to tell Kate, and there will be no reason for doing so if you will take my advice—which is, I need hardly tell you, to go and get married at once. Now that you have come into this money, your marrying becomes a positive duty. Are you aware that if you were run over and killed on your way home to-day Louise would have no standing? that she would not have a right to a penny of this money, or even to any of the furniture which is in your house? Let me see, how long is it that you have been"—he hesitated awkwardly—"together?"

Dering looked round at him rather fiercely. "We have been *married* nine years and a half," he said. "Our wedding day was the first of September. We spent our honeymoon in Denmark. You remember my little legacy?"

Wingfield nodded his head. His heart suddenly went out to his friend—the prosperous lawyer had reason to remember that hundred pounds legacy, for ten pounds of it had gone to help him out of some foolish scrape. But Dering had forgotten all that; he went on speaking, but more slowly:

"And then, as you know, we came back and settled down in Gray's Inn, and though we were horribly poor, perhaps poorer than even you ever guessed, we were divinely happy." He turned his back to the room and stared out once more at the greyness opposite.

"But you're quite right, old man, it's time we did like our betters! We'll be married at once, and I'll take her off for another and a longer honeymoon, and we'll come back and be even happier than we were before."

Then again, as abruptly as before, he was gone, shutting the door behind him, and leaving Wingfield staring thoughtfully after him.

That his friend, that the Philip Dering of ten years ago, should have done such a thing, was in no way remarkable, but that Louise—the thoughtful, well-balanced, intelligent woman, who, coming as a mere girl from Denmark, had known how to work her way up to a position of great trust and responsibility in a City house, so winning the esteem and confidence of her employers that they had again and again asked her to return to them after her marriage—that she should have consented to such—to such.... Wingfield even in his own mind hesitated for the right word ... to such an arrangement—seemed to the lawyer an astounding thing, savouring indeed of the fifth dimension.

No, no, he would certainly not tell Kate anything about it. Why should he? He knew very well how his wife would regard the matter, and how her condemnation would fall, not on Louise—Kate had become exceedingly fond of Louise—no, indeed, but on Dering. Kate had never cordially "taken" (a favourite word of hers, that) to Wingfield's friend; she thought him affected and unpractical, and she laughed at his turned-down collars and Liberty ties. No, no, there was no reason why Kate should be told a word of this extraordinary, this amazing story.

On leaving Abingdon Street, Philip Dering swung across the broad roadway, and made his way, almost instinctively, to the garden which lay so nearly opposite his friend's office windows. He wanted to calm down, to think things over, and to recover full possession of himself before going home.

It had cost him a considerable effort to tell Wingfield this thing. Not that he was in the least ashamed of what he and Louise had done—on the contrary, he was very proud of it—but he had often felt, during all those years, that he was being treacherous to the man who was, after all, his best friend; and there was in Dering enough of the feminine element—that element which Kate Wingfield so thoroughly despised in him—to make him feel sorry and ashamed.

However, Wingfield had taken it very well, just as he would have wished him to take it, and no doubt the lawyer had given thoroughly sound advice. This unexpected, this huge legacy made all the difference. Besides, Dering knew well enough, when he examined his own heart and conscience, that he felt very differently about all manner of things from what he had been wont to feel say ten years ago.

After all, he was following in the footsteps of men greater and wiser than he. It is impossible to be wholly consistent. If he had been consistent he would have refused to pay certain taxes—in fact, to have been wholly consistent during the last ten years would have probably landed him, England being what it is, in a lunatic asylum. He shuddered, suddenly remembering that for awhile his own mother had been insane.

Still, as he strode along the primly kept paths of the Thames-side garden, he felt a great and, as he thought, a legitimate pride in the knowledge that in this one all-important matter, so deeply affecting his own and Louise's life, he and she had triumphantly defied convention, and had come out victorious.

The young man's thoughts suddenly took a softer, a more intimate turn; he told himself, with intense secret satisfaction, that Louise was dearer, ay, far dearer and more indispensable to him now than she had been during the days when she was still the "sweet stranger whom he called his wife." He remembered once saying to Wingfield that the ideal mate should be the improbable, be able at once to clean a grate, to cook a dinner, and to discuss Ibsen! Well, Louise had more than fulfilled this early and rather absurd ideal.

From the day when they had first met and made unconventional acquaintance, with no intervening friend to form a gossip-link of introduction, Dering had found her full of ever-recurrent and enchanting surprises. Her foreign birth and upbringing gave her both original and unsuspected points of view about everything English, and he had often thought, with good-humoured pity, of all those unfortunate friends of his, Wingfield included, whose lot it had perforce been to choose their wives among their own country-women.

Dering had not seen much of Denmark, but everything he had seen had won his enthusiastic approval. Where else were modern women to be found at once so practical and so cultivated, so pure-minded and so large-hearted? Perhaps he was half aware that his heaven was of his own creation, but that, in his present exalted mood, was only an added triumph; how few human beings can evolve, and preserve at will, their own stretch of blue sky!

Of course it was not always as easy as it seemed to be to-day; lately Louise had been listless and tired, utterly unlike herself—even, he had once or twice thought with dismay, slightly hysterical! But all that would disappear, utterly, during the first few days of their coming travels; and even he, so he now reminded himself, had felt quite unlike his usual sensible self—Dering was very proud of his good sense—since had come the news of this wonderful, this fairy-gift-like legacy.

The young man passed out of the garden, his feet stepping from the soft shell-strewn gravel on to the wide pavement which borders the Houses of Parliament. He made his way round swiftly, each buoyant step a challenge to fate, to the Members' Entrance, and so across the road to the gate which leads into what was once the old parish churchyard of Westminster. It was still too cold to sit out of doors, and after a momentary hesitation he turned into Westminster Abbey by the great north door.

Dering had not been in the Abbey since he was a child, and the spirit of quietude which fills the broad nave and narrow aisles on early spring days soothed his restlessness. But that, alas! only for a moment; as soon as his busy brain began to realise all that lay about him, he was filled with a sincere if half voluntarily comic indignation. It annoyed him to feel that this national heritage was still a church; why could not Westminster Abbey be treated as are the Colosseum in Rome and the Panthéon in Paris? And so, as he sat down in one of the pews which roused his resentment, he began to think over all the improvements which he would effect, were he given, if only for a few days, a free hand in Westminster Abbey!

Suddenly he saw, at right angles with himself, and moving across the choir, a group of four people, consisting of a man, a woman, and two children.

The man was Jack Hinton, the idle, ill-conditioned artist neighbour of his in Bedford Park, to whom there had been more than one reference in his talk with Wingfield; the children were Agatha and Mary Hinton, the motherless girls of the Danish woman to whom Louise had been so much devoted; and the fourth figure was that of Louise herself. His wife's back was turned to Dering, but even without the other three he would have known the tall, graceful figure, if only by the masses of fair, almost lint-white hair, arranged in low coils below her neat hat.

Dering felt no wish to join the little party. He was still too excited, too interested in his own affairs, to care for making and hearing small talk. Still, a look of satisfaction came over his face as he watched the four familiar figures finally disappear round a pillar. How pleased Louise would be when he told her of his latest scheme, that of commissioning the unfortunate Hinton to paint her portrait! If only the man could be induced to work, he might really make something of his life after all. Dering meant to give the artist one hundred pounds, and his heart glowed at the thought of what such a sum would mean in the untidy, womanless little house in which his wife took so tender and kindly an interest.

Dering and Jack Hinton had never exactly hit it off together, though they had known each other for many years, and though they had both married Danish wives. The one felt for the other the worker's worldly contempt for the incorrigible idler. Yet, Dering had been very sorry for Hinton at the time of poor Mrs. Hinton's death, and he liked to think that now he would be able to do the artist a good turn. He had even thought very seriously of offering to adopt the youngest Hinton child, a baby now nearly a year old; but a certain belated feeling of prudence, of that common sense which often tempers the wind to the reckless enthusiast, had given him pause.

After all, he and Louise might have children of their own, and then the position of this little interloper might be an awkward one. Louise had always intensely wished to have a child—nay, children—and now, if it only depended on him, and if Nature would only be kind, she should have her wish. Perhaps that would be the most tangible good this legacy would bring them.

Dering left the Abbey by the door which gives access to the Cloisters. There he spent half an hour in pleasant meditation before he started home, for the place which he knew to be so much dearer to his wife than to himself. Dering was a Londoner, the son of a doctor who had practised for many years in one of the City parishes, and in his heart he had much preferred the rooms in Gray's Inn which had been their first married home to the trim little villa, of which the interior had acquired an absurd and touching resemblance to that of a Danish homestead.

Those who declare that the borderlands of London lack physiognomy are strangely mistaken. Each suburban district has an individual character of its own, and of none is this more true than of Bedford Park. Encompassed by poor and populous streets, within a stone's throw of what is still one of the great highways out of the town, this oasis, composed of villas set in gardens, has the tranquil, rather mysterious, charm of a river backwater.

The amazing contrast between the stir and unceasing sound of the broad High Road and the stillness of Lady Rich Road—surely the man who laid out Bedford Park must have been a Cromwell enthusiast—struck Dering with a sense of unwonted pleasure. As he put his latch-key in the front door he remembered that his wife had told him that their young Danish servant was to have that day her evening out. Well, so much the better; they would have their talk, their discussion concerning their future plans, without fear of eavesdropping or interruption.

Various little signs showed that Louise was already back from town. Dering went straight upstairs, and, as he began taking off his boots, he called out to her, though the door between his room and hers was shut: "Do come in here, for I have so much to tell you!" But this brought no answering word, and after a moment he heard his wife's soft footsteps going down the house.

Dering dressed himself with some care; it had always been one of his theories that a man should make himself quite as formally agreeable at home as he does elsewhere, and he and Louise had ever practised, the one to the other, the minor courtesies of life. Before going downstairs he also tidied his room, as far as was possible for him to do so, and, delicately picking up his dusty boots, he took them down into the kitchen so as to save their young servant the trouble.

Then, at last, he went through into the dining-room, where he found Louise standing by the table on which lay spread their simple supper.

She gave him a quick, questioning glance, then: "I saw you in the Abbey," she said in a constrained, hesitating voice; "why did you not come up and speak to us? Mr. Hinton was on his way to some office, and I brought the children back alone."

"If I had known that was going to be the case," said Dering frankly, "I should have joined you, but I had just been spending an hour with Wingfield, and—well, I didn't feel in the mood to make small talk for Hinton!"

He waited a moment, but she made no comment.

Louise had always been a silent, listening woman, and this had made her seem, to eager, ardent Philip, a singularly restful companion.

He went on, happily at first, rather nervously towards the close of his sentence, "Well, everything is settled—even to my will. But I found Wingfield had to know—I mean about our old arrangement."

"Then you told him? I do not think you should have done that." Louise spoke very slowly, and in a low voice. "I asked you if I might do so before telling Gerda Hinton."

Dering looked at her deprecatingly. He felt both surprised and sorry. It was almost the first time in their joint lives that she had uttered to him anything savouring of a rebuke.

"Please forgive my having told Wingfield without first consulting you," he said at once; "but you see the absurd, the abominable state of the English law is such that in case of my sudden death you would have no right to any of this money. Besides, apart from that fact, if I trusted to my own small legal knowledge and made a will in which you were mentioned, you would probably have trouble with those odious relations of mine. So I simply had to tell him."

Dering saw that the discussion was beginning to be very painful and disagreeable; he felt a pang of impatient regret that he had spoken to his wife now, instead of waiting until she had had a thorough change and holiday.

Louise was still standing opposite to him, looking straight before her and avoiding his anxious glances. Suddenly he became aware that her lip was trembling, and that her eyes were full of tears; quickly he walked round to where she was standing, and put his hand on her shoulder.

"I am sorry, very sorry, that I had to tell Wingfield," he said; "but, darling, why should you mind so much? He was quite sympathetic; he thoroughly understood; I think I might even say that he thoroughly agrees with our point of view; but I fancy he felt rather hurt about it, and I couldn't help wishing that we had told him at the time."

Dering's hand travelled from his wife's shoulder to her waist, and he held her to him, unresisting but strangely passive, as he added:

"You can guess, my dearest, what Wingfield, in his character of solicitor, advises us to do? Of course, in a sense it will be a fall from grace,—but, after all, we shan't love one another the less because we have been to a registry office, or spent a quarter of an hour in a church! I do think that we should follow his advice. He will let me know to-morrow what formalities have to be fulfilled to carry the thing through, and then, dear heart, we will go off for a second honeymoon. Sometimes I wonder if you realise what this money means to us both—I mean in the way of freedom and of added joy."

But Louise still turned from him, and, as she disengaged herself from the strong encircling arm, he could see the slow, reluctant tears rolling down her cheek.

Dering felt keenly distressed. The long strain, the gallantly endured poverty, the constant anxiety, had evidently told on his wife more than he had known.

"Don't let's talk about it any more!" he exclaimed. "There's no hurry about it now, after all."

"I would rather talk about it now, Philip. I don't—I don't at all understand what you mean. It is surely too late for us now to talk of marriage. The time remaining to us is too short to make it worth while."

Dering looked at her bewildered. Well as she spoke the language, she had remained very ignorant of England and of English law.

"I will try and explain to you," he said gently, "why Wingfield has made it quite clear to me that we shall have to go through some kind of a legal ceremony——"

"But there are so few months," she repeated, and he felt her trembling; "it is not as if you were likely to die before September; besides, if you were to do so, I should not care about the money."

For the first time a glimmer of what she meant, of what she was thinking, came into Dering's mind. He felt strongly moved and deeply touched. This, then, was why she had seemed so preoccupied, so unlike herself, of late.

"My darling, surely you do not imagine—that I am thinking ... of leaving you?"

"No," and for the first time Louise, as she uttered the word, looked up straight into Dering's face. "No, it was not of you that I was thinking—but of myself...."

"Let us sit down." Dering's voice was so changed, so uneager, so cold, that Louise, for the first time during their long partnership, felt as if she was with a stranger. "I want to thoroughly understand your point of view. Do you mean to say that when we first arranged matters you intended our—our marriage to be, in any case, only a temporary union?"

He waited for an answer, looking at her with a still grimness, an unfamiliar antagonism, that raised in her a feeling of resentment, and renewed her courage. "Please tell me," he said again, "I think you owe me the truth, and I really wish to know."

Then she spoke. And though her hands still trembled, her voice was quite steady.

"Yes, Philip, I will tell you the truth, though I fear you will not like to hear it. When I first accepted the proposal you made to me, I felt convinced that, as regarded myself, the feeling which brought us together would be eternal, but I as fully believed that with you that same feeling would be only temporary. I was ready to remain with you as long as you would have me do so; but I felt sure that you would grow tired of me some day, and I told myself—secretly, of course, for I could not have insulted you or myself by saying such a thing to you then—I told myself, I say, that when that day came, the day of your weariness of me, I would go away, and make no further demand upon you."

"You really believed that I should grow tired of you,—that I should wish to leave you?"

Dering looked at her as a man might look at a stranger who has suddenly revealed some sinister and grotesque peculiarity of appearance or manner.

"Certainly I did so. How could I divine that you alone would be different from all the men of whom I had ever heard? Still, I loved you so well—ah, Philip, I did love you so—that I would have come to you on any terms, as indeed I did come on terms very injurious to myself. But what matters now what I then thought? I see that I was wrong—you have been faithful to me in word, thought, and deed——"

"Yes," said Dering fiercely, "by God, that is so! Go on!"

"I also have been faithful to you——" she hesitated. "Yes, I think I may truly say it, in thought, word, and deed,——"

Dering drew a long breath, and she went slowly on: "But I have realised, and that for some time past, that the day would come when I should no longer wish to be so—when I should wish to be free. I have gradually regained possession of myself, and, though I know I must fulfil all my obligations to you for the time I promised, I long for the moment of release, for the moment when I shall at last have the right to forget, as much as such things can ever be forgotten, these ten years of my life."

As she spoke, pronouncing each word clearly in the foreign fashion, her voice gained a certain sombre confidence, and a flood of awful, hopeless bitterness filled the heart of the man sitting opposite to her.

"And have you thought," he asked in a constrained voice, "what you are going to do? I know you have sometimes regretted your work; do you intend—or perhaps you have already applied to Mr. Farningham?"

"No," she answered, and, unobserved by him, for he was staring down at the tablecloth with unseeing eyes, a deep pink flush made her look suddenly girlish, "that will not be necessary. I have, as you know, regretted my work, and of late I have sometimes thought that, things being as they were, you acted with cruel thoughtlessness in compelling me to give it all up. But in my new life there will be much for me to do."

"I do not ask you," he said, suddenly, hoarsely; "I could not insult you by asking...."

"I do not think," she spoke slowly, answering the look, the intonation, rather than the words, "that I am going to do anything unworthy."

But Dering, with sharp suspicion, suddenly became aware that she had changed colour, and that from pale she had become red. His mind glanced quickly over their comparatively small circle of friends and acquaintances—first one, then another familiar figure rose, hideously vivid, before him. He felt helpless, bewildered, fettered.

"Do you contemplate leaving me for another man?" he asked quietly.

Again Louise hesitated for a moment.

"Yes," she said at length, "that is what I am going to do. I did not mean to tell you now—though I admit that later, before the end, you would have had a right to know. The man to whom I am going, and who is not only willing, but anxious, to make me his wife, I mean his legal wife,"—she gave Dering a quick, strange look—"has great need of me, far more so than you ever had. My feeling for him is not in any way akin to what was once my feeling for you; that does not come twice, at any rate to such a woman as I feel myself to be; but my affection, my—my regard, will be, in this case, I believe, more enduring; and, as you know, I dearly love his children, and promised their mother to take care of them."

While she spoke, Dering, looking fixedly at her, seemed to see a shadowy group of shabby forlorn human beings form itself and take up its stand by her side—Jack Hinton, with his weak, handsome face, and shifty, pleading eyes; his two plain, neglected-looking girls; and then, cradled as he had so often seen it in Louise's arms, the ugly and to him repulsive-looking baby.

What chance had he, what memories had their common barren past, to fight this intangible appealing vision?

He raised his hand and held it for a moment over his eyes, in a vain attempt to shut out both that which he had evoked, and the sight of the woman whose repudiation of himself only seemed to make more plainly visible the bonds which linked them the one to the other. Then he turned away, with a certain deliberation, and, having closed the door, walked quickly through the little hall, flinging himself bare-headed into the open air.

For the second time that day Philip Dering felt an urgent need of solitude in which to hold communion with himself. And yet, when striding along the dimly-lighted, solitary thoroughfares, the stillness about him seemed oppressive, and the knowledge that he was encompassed by commonplace, contented folk intolerable.

And so, scarcely knowing where his feet were leading him, he made his way at last into the broad, brilliantly lighted High Road, now full of glare, of sound, and of movement, for throngs of workers, passing to and fro, were seeking the amusement and excitement of the street after their long, dull day.

Very soon Dering's brain became abnormally active; his busy thoughts took the shape of completed half-uttered sentences, and he argued with himself, not so loudly that those about him could hear, but still with moving lips, as to the outcome of what Louise had told him that evening.

He was annoyed to find that his thoughts refused to marshal themselves in due sequence. Thus, when trying to concentrate his mind on the question of the immediate future, memories of Gerda Hinton, of the dead woman with whom he had never felt in sympathy, perhaps because Louise had been so fond of her, persistently intervened, and refused to be thrust away. His own present intolerable anguish made him, against his will, retrospectively understand Gerda's long-drawn-out agony. He remembered, with new sharp-edged concern and pity, her quiet endurance of those times of ignoble poverty brought about by Hinton's fits of idleness; he realised for the first time what must have meant, in anguish of body and mind, the woman's perpetual child bearing, and the deaths of two of her children, followed by her own within a fortnight of her last baby's birth.

Then, with sudden irritation, he asked himself why he, Philip Dering, should waste his short time for thought in sorrowing over this poor dead woman? And, in swift answer, there came to him the knowledge why this sad drab ghost had thus thrust herself upon him to-night—

A feeling of furious anger, of revolt against the very existence of Jack Hinton, swept over him. So base, so treacherous, so selfish a creature fulfilled no useful purpose in the universe. Men hung murderers; and was Hinton, who had done his wife to death with refinement of cruelty, to go free—free to murder, in the same slow way, another woman, and one who actually belonged to Dering's own self?

He now recognised, with bewilderment, that had Louise become his legal wife ten years ago, the thought of what she proposed to do would never have even crossed her mind.

The conviction that Hinton was not fit to live soon formed itself into a stable background to all Dering's subsequent thoughts, to his short hesitations, and to his final determination.

After a while he looked at his watch, and found, with some surprise, that he had been walking up and down for over an hour; he also became aware, for the first time, that his bare, hatless head provoked now and again good-natured comment from those among whom he was walking.

He turned into a side-street, and taking from his pocket a small notebook, wrote the few lines which later played an important part in determining, to the satisfaction of his friends, the fact that he was, when writing them, most probably of unsound mind.

What Dering wrote down in his pocket-book ran as follows:

> 1. I buy a hat at Dunn's, if Dunn be still open (which is probable).
>
> 2. I call on the doctor who was so kind to the Hintons last year and settle his account. It is doubtful if Hinton ever paid him—in fact, there can be no doubt that Hinton did *not* pay him. I there make my will and inform the doctor that he will certainly be wanted shortly at Number 8, Lady Rich Road.

3. I buy that revolver (if guaranteed in perfect working order) which I have so frequently noticed in the pawnbroker's window, and I give him five shillings for showing me how to manage it. Mem. Remember to make him load it, so that there may be no mistake.

4. I wire to Wingfield. This is important. It may save Louise a shock.

5. I go to Hinton's place, and if the children are already in bed I lock the door, and quietly kill him and then kill myself. If the children are still up, I must, of course, wait a while. In any case the business will be well over before the doctor can arrive.

Dering shut the notebook with a sigh of relief. The way now seemed clear before him, for he had put down exactly what he meant to do, and in case of doubt or forgetfulness he need only glance at his notes to be set again in the right way.

He spent a few moments considering whether it was his duty to write a letter to his employer. Finally he decided that there was no need to do so. They knew of his legacy; they were aware that he was leaving them; and everything, even now, was in perfect order for his successor.

As he walked slowly along the unlovely narrow streets which run parallel to the High Road, his emotional memory brought his wife vividly before him. He began wondering painfully if she would ever understand, if she would realise, from what he had saved her by that which he was about to do. His knowledge of her character made him feel sure—and there was infinite comfort in the thought—that she would remain silent, that she would never yield to any foolish impulse to tell Wingfield the truth. It was good to feel so sure that his old friend would never know of his failure, of his great and desolate humiliation.

Dering spent the next hour exactly as he had planned; in fact, at no point of the programme did his good fortune desert him. Thus, even the doctor, a man called Johnstone, who might so easily have been out, was at home; and, though actually giving a little stag party, he good-naturedly consented to leave his guests for a few moments, in spite of the fact that the stranger waiting in the surgery had refused to state his business.

"My name is Dering. I think you must have often met my wife when you were attending the late Mrs. Hinton. In fact I've come to-night to settle the Hintons' account. I fancy it is still owing?"

Dering spoke with abrupt energy, looking straight, and almost with a frown, as he spoke, into the other's kindly florid face. It seemed strange, at that moment intolerably hard, that this man, who looked so much less alive, so much less intellectually keen than himself, should be destined to find him within a few hours lying dead, obliterated into nothingness.

"Oh, yes, the account is still owing," Dr. Johnstone spoke with a certain eagerness. "Then do I understand that you are acting for Mr. Hinton in the matter? The amount is exactly ten pounds——"

He paused awkwardly, and not till the two bank-notes were actually lying on his surgery table before him did he believe in his good fortune. The Hintons' account had long since passed into that class of doctor's bills which is only kept on the books with a view to the ultimate sale of the practice, and this last quarter the young man had not even troubled to send it in again.

Johnstone remembered poor Mrs. Hinton's friend very well; Mrs. Dering had been splendid, perfectly splendid, as nurse and comforter to the distracted household. And then such a pretty woman, too, the very type—quiet, sensible, self-contained, and yet feminine—whom Dr. Johnstone admired; he was always pleased when he met her walking about the neighbourhood.

This, then, was her husband? The doctor stared across at Dering with some curiosity. Well, he also, though, of course, in quite another way, was uncommon and attractive-looking. What was it he had heard about these people quite lately, in fact, that very day? Why, of course. One of his old lady patients in Bedford Park had told him that her opposite neighbours, this Mr. and Mrs. Dering, had come into a large fortune—something like fifty thousand pounds!

Dr. Johnstone looked at his visitor with a sudden accession of respect. If he could have foreseen this interview, he might have made his account with Mr. Hinton bear rather more relation to the actual number of visits he had been compelled to pay to that unfortunate household. Still, he reminded himself that even ten pounds were very welcome just now, and his heart warmed to Mr. Hinton's generous friend.

Suddenly Dering began speaking: "I forget if I told you that I am starting this very night for a long journey, and before doing so I want to ask you to do me a favour——"

His host became all pleased attention.

"Would you kindly witness my will? I have just come into a sum of money, and—and, though my will is actually being drawn up by a friend, who is also a lawyer, I have felt uneasy——"

"I quite understand. You have thought it wise to make a provisional will? Well, that's a very sensible thing to do! We medical men see much trouble caused by foolish postponement of such matters. Some men seem to think that making a will is tantamount to signing their own death-warrant!"

But no answering smile brightened Dering's fiercely set face; he did not seem to have heard what the doctor had said. "If I might ask you for a sheet of notepaper. I see a pen and blotting-pad over there——"

A sudden, instinctive misgiving crossed the other's mind.

"This is rather informal, isn't it? Of course, I have no call to interfere, Mr. Dering; but if a large sum is involved might it not be better to wait?"

Dering looked up. For the first time he smiled.

"I don't wish to make any mystery about it, Dr. Johnstone. I am leaving everything to my wife, and after her to sundry young people in whom we are both interested. If I die intestate, I understand that distant relatives of my own—people whom I don't like, and who have never done anything for me—are bound to benefit."

Even as he spoke he was busy writing the words, "To Louise Larsen (commonly known as Mrs. Philip Dering), of 9, Lady Rich Road, Bedford Park, and after her death to be divided equally between the children of my esteemed friend, James Wingfield, solicitor, of 24, Abingdon Street, Westminster, and the children of the late Mrs. John Hinton, of 8, Lady Rich Road, Bedford Park."

Short as was Dering's will, the last portion of it was written on the inner sheet of the piece of note paper bearing the doctor's address, and the two witnesses, Johnstone himself, and a friend whom he fetched out of his smoking-room for the purpose, could not help seeing what generous provision the testator had made for the younger generation.

As the doctor opened the front door for his, as he hoped, new friend, Dering suddenly pulled a notebook out of his breast pocket.

"I have forgotten a most important thing——" there was real dismay in his fresh, still youthful voice—"and that is to ask you kindly to look round at No. 8, Lady Rich Road, after your friends have left you to-night. I should think about twelve o'clock would do very well. In fact, Hinton won't be ready for you before. And, Dr. Johnstone—in view of the trouble to which you may be put——" Dering thrust another bank-note into the other man's hand. "I know you ought to have charged a lot more than that ten pounds———" and then, before words of thanks could be uttered, he had turned and gone down the steps, along the little path, through the iron gate which swung under the red lamp, into the darkness beyond.

Down the broad and now solitary High Road, filled with the strange brooding stillness of a spring dawn, clattered discordantly a hansom cab. There was promise of a bright warm day, such a day as yesterday had been, but Wingfield, leaning forward, unconsciously willing the horse to go faster, felt very cold.

At last, not for the first time during this interminable journey, he took from his breast pocket the unsigned telegram which was the cause of his being here, driving, oh! how slowly, along this fantastically empty thoroughfare, through the chill morning air, instead of lying sound asleep by Kate's side in his comfortable bed at home.

"*Philip Dering is dead please come at once at once at once to eight Lady Rich Road.*"

Wingfield, steadying the slip of paper as it fluttered in his hand, looked down with frowning puzzled eyes at the pencilled words.

The message had been set off just before midnight, and had reached his house, he supposed, an hour and a half later, for the persistent knocking at his front door had gone on for some time before he or his wife realised that the loud hammering sound concerned themselves. Even then it had been Kate who had at last roused herself and gone downstairs; Kate who had rushed up breathless, whispering as she thrust the orange envelope into his hand:—"Oh, James, what can it be? Thank God, all the children are safe at home!"

No time had been lost. While he was dressing, his wife had made him a cup of tea, kind and solicitous for his comfort, but driving him nearly distracted by her eager, excited talk and aimless conjectures. It had seemed long before he found a derelict cab willing to drive him from Regent's Terrace to Bedford Park, but now—well, thank God, he was at last nearing the place where he would learn what had befallen the man who had been, next to his own elder boy, the creature he had loved best in his calm, phlegmatic life.

Wingfield went on staring down at the mysterious and yet explicit message, of which the wording seemed to him so odd—in some ways recalling Dering's familiar trick of reiteration. Then suddenly he thought of Hinton, the artist for whom both he and his friend had had reason to feel so deep if wordless a contempt, and yet whom they had both tried, over and over again, to help and set on his feet.

With a sudden revulsion of feeling, the lawyer folded up the telegram and put it back into his breast pocket—this mysterious, unsigned request for his immediate presence had obviously been despatched by Hinton, who might just as well have waited for morning. How stupid of him not to have realised this at once, the more so that No. 8, Lady Rich Road, was Hinton's address, not that of Dering. Quickly he raised his hand to the trap-door above his head; "Pull up at No. 8, not as I told you, at No. 9, Lady Rich Road," he shouted.

The radiance of an early spring morning, so kind to everything in nature, is pitiless to that which owes its being to the ingenuity and industry of human hands. Dr. Johnstone, standing opposite a police inspector in what had been poor Mrs. Hinton's cherished, if untidy and shabby, little sitting-room, felt his wretchedness and shame—for he felt very deeply ashamed—perceptibly increased by the dust-laden sunbeams dancing slantwise about him.

The inspector was really sorry for him, though a little contemptuous perhaps of a medical man capable of showing such emotion and horror in the face of death.

"Why, doctor, you mustn't take on so! How could you possibly have told what was in the man's mind? You weren't upset like this last year over that business in Angle Alley, and that was a sight worse than this, eh?"

But Johnstone had turned away, and was staring out of the bow window. "It isn't that poor wretch Hinton that's upset me," he muttered, "I don't mind death. It's—it's—Dering—Dering and Mrs. Dering." Reluctant tears filled his tired, red-rimmed eyes.

"I'm sorry, too. Very sorry for the lady, that is; as for the other—well, I'm pretty sure he'll cheat Broadmoor, and that without much delay, eh, doctor? Hullo! who's this coming now?"

The tone suddenly changed, became at once official and alert in quality, as the sound of wheels stopped opposite the little gate. When the front door bell pealed through the house he added, "You go to the door, doctor; whoever it is had better not see me at first." And Johnstone found himself suddenly pushed out of the room and into the little hall.

There he hesitated for a moment, looking furtively round at the half-open door which led into the back room fitted up as a studio, where still lay, in dreadful juxtaposition, the dead and the dying, Hinton and his murderer, alone, save for the indifferent yet watchful presence of a trained nurse.

From the kitchen beyond came the sound of eager, lowered voices, those of the two young servants who had of late coped with the difficulties of the Hinton household, and whose scanty wages had been paid, so Johnstone had learned in the last hour, by Mrs. Dering herself.

Another impatient peal of sound echoed through the house, and the doctor, walking slowly forward, opened the front door.

"Can I see Mr. Hinton? Or is he next door? I have driven down from town in response to this telegram. I was Mr. Philip Dering's oldest friend and solicitor——"

"Then—then it was *you* who were making his will?"

The question struck Wingfield as unseemly. How had this young man, whom he took to be one of Hinton's dissipated friends, learnt even this one fact concerning poor Dering's affairs?

"Yes," he said shortly, as he walked through into the hall, "that was the case. But, of course—well, perhaps, you will kindly inform me where I can see Mr. Hinton?" he repeated impatiently. "I suppose he is with Mrs. Dering, at No. 9?" and the other noticed that he left the door open behind him, evidently intending to leave Hinton's house as soon as he had obtained a reply to his question.

For a moment the two men looked at one another in exasperated silence. Then, very suddenly, Johnstone did that of which he was afterward sorry and self-reproachful. But his nerve was completely gone; for hours he had been engaged in what had proved both a terrible and a futile task, that of attempting to relieve the physical agony of a man for whose state he partly held himself to be responsible. He wished to avoid, at any rate for the present, the repetition to this stranger of what had happened the night before.

And so, "Please come this way," he muttered hoarsely. "I ought perhaps to warn you—to prepare you for something of a shock." And, turning round, beckoning to the other to follow him, he opened the door of the studio, stepping aside to allow Wingfield to pass in before him.

But once through the doorway the lawyer suddenly recoiled and stopped short, so dreadful and so unexpected was the sight which met his eyes.

What Wingfield saw remained with him for weeks, and even for months, an ever-present, torturing vision, full of mingled horror and mystery, a mystery to which he was destined never to find the solution.

Focussed against a blurred background made up of distempered light green walls, a curtainless, open window, and various plain deal studio properties pushed back against the wall, lay, stretched out on some kind of low couch brought forward into the middle of the room, a rigid, motionless figure.

The lower half of the figure, including the feet, which rested on a chair placed at the bottom of the couch, was entirely covered by a blanket; but the chest and head, slightly raised by pillows, seemed swathed and bound up in broad strips of white linen, which concealed chin and forehead, hair and ears, while the head was oddly supported by a broad band or sling fastened with safety-pins—Wingfield's eyes took note of every detail—to the side of the couch. Under the blanket, which was stretched tightly across the man's breast, could be seen the feeble twitching of fingers, but even so, the only sense of life and feeling seemed to the onlooker centred in the eyes, whose glance Wingfield found himself fearing yet longing to meet.

To the right of the couch a large Japanese screen had been so placed as to hide some object spread out on the floor. To the left, watching every movement of the still, recumbent figure, stood a powerful-looking woman in nursing dress. Wingfield's gaze, after wandering round the large, bare room, returned and again clung to the sinister immobile form which he longed to be told was that of Hinton, and as he gazed he forced himself to feel a fierce gladness and relief in the knowledge that Dering was dead,— that in his pocket lay the telegram which proved it.

At last, to gain courage and to stifle a horrible doubt, he compelled himself to meet those at once indifferent and appealing eyes, which seemed to stare fixedly beyond the group of men by the door; and suddenly the lawyer became aware that just behind him hurried whispered words were being uttered.

"This gentleman is Mr. Dering's solicitor; perhaps he will be able to throw some light on the whole affair," and he felt himself being plucked by the sleeve and gently pulled back into the hall.

"It is—isn't it?—poor Hinton?" and he looked imploringly from one man to the other.

"Hinton?" said the doctor sharply. "He's there, sure enough—but you didn't see him, for we put him under a sheet, behind that screen. Your friend shot him dead first, and then cut his own throat, but he didn't set about that in quite the right way, so he's alive still, as you can see."

Wingfield drew a long breath of something like relief. The torturing suspense of the last few moments was at an end.

"And where is Mrs. Dering?" he spoke in a quiet, mechanical voice; and Johnstone felt angered by his callousness.

"We've just sent her back into the next house," he answered curtly, "and made her take the Hinton children with her. For—well, it often is so in such cases, you know—the presence of his wife seems positively to distress Mr. Dering; besides, the nurse and I can do, and have done, all that is possible."

"And have you no clue to what has happened? Has Dering been able to give no explanation of this—this—horrible business?"

Johnstone shook his head. "Of course he can't speak. He will never speak again. He wrote a few words to his wife, but they amounted to nothing save regret that he had bungled the last half of the affair."

"And what do you yourself think?"

Wingfield spoke calmly and authoritatively. He had suddenly become aware, during the last few moments, that he was talking to a medical man.

"I haven't had time to think much about it;" the tone was rough and sore. "Mr. Dering seems to have come into a large sum of money, and such things have been known to upset men's brains before now."

"Still, he might write something of consequence, now that this gentleman has come," interposed the inspector.

But when Wingfield, standing by that which he now knew was indeed his friend, watched the painful, laboured moving of the pencil across the slate which had been hurriedly fetched some two hours before from the young Hintons' nursery, all he saw, traced again and again, were the words:

"Look after Louise. Look after Louise ..." and then at last: "I mean to die. I mean to die. I mean to die."

V

SHAMEFUL BEHAVIOUR?

"Yes; there; wives be such a provoking class of society, because though they be never right, they be never more than half wrong."—THE TRANTER in *Under the Greenwood Tree*.

I

The fact that it was Mrs. Rigby's Silver Wedding Day, and that she was now awaiting her only brother who was to be the fourth at the dinner she and her husband, the respected Town Clerk of Market Dalling, were giving in honour of the event, appeared to her no reason why she should sit in her parlour with hands idle in her lap. There was a large work-basket on a table close to her elbow, and with quick, capable fingers she was engaged in mending a pillow-case.

It was late June, and Mrs. Rigby sat by the widely open French windows which gave access to her garden—one of those fragrant walled gardens which still embellish the rear of the High Street in a very typically English market town.

Now and again the work would drop between her hands, and lie unheeded on her knee, while she looked out, focussing her dark, bright eyes on the distant figure of a woman who sat in a summer-house situated at the extreme end of the garden; and as Mrs. Rigby gazed thoughtfully at this, her other wedding guest, her whole face would soften—so might a mother look at a daughter whom instinct prompted her to love, and reason to condemn as foolish.

And yet the sitting figure was that of a contemporary of Mrs. Rigby, being, as a matter of fact, a certain Matilda Wellow, who had been her bridesmaid twenty-five years ago to-day, and who was now, in more than one sense of the term, the most substantial spinster of Market Dalling.

The sound of the door behind her quietly opening and shutting made Mrs. Rigby turn round, and a moment later she was looking up at a tall, straight, still young-looking man, who, clad in evening dress, stood smiling down at her. He was David Banfield, her half-brother.

"Why, you've put on all your war-paint!" she exclaimed in half-pretended dismay. "Didn't you know that there was only Matilda Wellow coming?"

"I don't know that I thought anything about it," he answered, more gaily than his sister was now in the habit of hearing him speak. "I dressed out of compliment to you, Kate, and because—well, I've got into the way of it lately. But pray don't let Matt think that he must needs follow my example!"

Then he sat down by Mrs. Rigby, and gazed out with quick, sensitive appreciation at the old walled garden.

"You're a wonderful gardener, Kate," he said suddenly.

"There's a lot of nonsense talked now about gardening," she said drily. "With the grand ladies you see such a lot of, Dave, it's just a passing fad."

Her brother made no answer; he looked down at her with uncritical and yet dissatisfied eyes. She was a handsome woman, and even now only forty-six, and yet she managed to convey an impression of age. This was partly owing to her unsuitable dress, for Mrs. Rigby was wearing a dark blue silk gown, chosen, not only to grace her silver wedding day, but also with a view to being her best dress during the coming autumn and winter.

Kate Rigby loved her half-brother, David Banfield, as only a childless woman can love the creature to whom she has stood for long years in the place of mother. David was twelve years younger than herself, and, with one exception, he had never caused her a moment's real unhappiness or unease. The exception, however, had been paramount, for with him had been connected Mrs. Rigby's only taste of sharp pain and sorrow, and, worse still, to such a woman as herself, of disgrace.

The young man's marriage to an Irish singer, which had taken place without his sister's knowledge, had proved disastrous. Rosaleen Tara—to give her the stage name by which her charming rendering of the old national ballads had made her widely known—had never liked, or been suited to, life as led at Market Dalling; and to make matters worse, she was a Roman Catholic.

After a few years' unsatisfactory married life, and the birth of one child, a girl, Mrs. David Banfield had returned, with her husband's grudging consent, to the musical stage. Then, on the very day Banfield had been expecting his wife home for a short holiday, there had come from her a letter telling him shortly, bluntly, cruelly, that she had been unfaithful to her marriage vow, and that she hoped he would forget her.

Had he forgotten her? No. It had only been owing to his sister's urgency, and to Matthew Rigby's more measured advice, that Banfield had at last consented to take the step of divorcing his wife.

This step Mrs. Rigby had not only never regretted, but—and in this she was more fortunate than her husband—no doubt had ever crossed her mind of its having been the wisest thing for her brother's happiness and peace. But Matthew Rigby, cautious member of a cautious profession, had learned very early in his married life the futility of disagreeing with the wife with whom Providence had blessed him.

Now Banfield lived in solitary state with his little girl, his household managed by the child's nurse, an old Irishwoman, who, if devoted to the child, was incapable of managing such a decorous household as should have been that of the Brew House.

Any day, any hour, Mrs. Rigby would have bartered her personal happiness for that of her half-brother, and yet the two seldom met—and they met almost daily—without the saying on her part of something likely either to wound or to annoy him.

"I suppose Rosy is well? I thought you meant sending the child in to see me to-day?"

"Didn't she come?" A look of worry and anger crossed Banfield's dark, mobile face. "I can't think what prevented it, unless—well, there's been rather an upset at the Brew House, and perhaps Mary Scanlan didn't like to go out."

"I heard there had been an upset," observed his sister drily, "for baker told cook. He said your housekeeper turned the younger maid, old Hornby's daughter, out of the house last night, and that the girl could be heard crying all down the street."

Mrs. Rigby let her work fall unheeded on the floor; quite unconscious of her action she clasped her hands tightly together.

"David! How long is this sort of thing to go on?" she asked, in a low, tense voice. "It's the talk of the whole town, and it can't be good for your child."

"But what would you have me do?" He had hoped that to-day—his sister's silver wedding day—his domestic trials would be forgotten, or, at any rate, not mentioned. "I can't dismiss Mary Scanlan now—she must stay on till Rosy goes to school. That won't be for very long, for, as you know, I promised"—he averted his face as he spoke—"to send the child to a convent school as soon as she was twelve years old."

The idea that her brother, the wealthy, highly-thought-of brewer of Market Dalling, should confess himself worsted by the old and ill-tempered Irishwoman, who, together with little Rosy, had been his wife's—his unfaithful wife's—only legacy to him, was horrible to his sister.

Even now, when bitter, disconnected thoughts crowded one on another, Mrs. Rigby, half-unconsciously, evoked in her mind the strong personality of the one human being who ever really "stood up" to her. She had had the notion, so curiously common in England, that your Irishwoman is invariably slatternly, untruthful, and good-natured; but in Mary Scanlan she had found a human being as scrupulously neat, truthful, and high-minded as herself, while at the same time far more ill-tempered, and equally determined to have her own way.

While Mrs. Rigby was allowing a flood of very bitter thoughts to surge up round her, David Banfield was watching her face, and awaiting her next words with some anxiety.

But when Kate Rigby at last spoke, she seemed to have forgotten the immediate question under discussion.

"I suppose," she said slowly, "that you have never thought, Dave, that there might be a simple way out of your difficulties?"

"You mean that I might marry again? Well, Kate, yes—I have thought of it. I suppose there's no man, situated as I have been these last four years, but thinks of a second marriage as a way out; but—but, apart from other considerations, I don't feel as if I could bring myself to do it."

"And why not, pray?" asked Mrs. Rigby in a low voice.

"Well, it's difficult to explain the way I look at it. Of course, no one can answer for another, and yet, Kate, if anything happened to Matt, I don't see you marrying again———?"

David Banfield was aware that he had not chosen a very happy simile with which to point his meaning, and perhaps, in his heart of hearts, he hoped that what he had said would put an end to a painful discussion. But any such hope was destined to be grievously disappointed, for his sister, with suddenly heightened colour, turned on him very sharply.

"Don't talk nonsense!" she exclaimed. "I'm an old woman, and you're a young man!" and she set back her vigorous, powerful shoulders.

"You know very well that if Matthew had dared to treat me as you were treated by Rosal———" something in her brother's face caused his wife's name to die away on her lips—"I should have felt myself free to do exactly what suited me best! Surely, when you go out among your grand county friends, you must meet nice young ladies who would be only too pleased to become Mrs. David Banfield, and to step into such a home as the Brew House?"

Mrs. Rigby looked eagerly, furtively, at her brother.

The way in which he had been welcomed, to a certain extent absorbed, in the rather dull county society round Market Dalling, had been, to his sister, a source of mingled pride and jealousy, the more so that it had begun in the days of his pretty wife, whose modest professional fame had preceded her, and made her a welcome addition to county gatherings and dinner-parties. Then had come the great break of the war, and in South Africa Banfield had been naturally thrown with the landowners of his own part of the world.

So it was that during the first few months which had followed on his return home, Mrs. Rigby had fully expected her brother to make another, maybe as disastrous a matrimonial experiment as before, and in a class which was as little his own as that of his Irish wife had been.

But time had gone on, and David Banfield had shown no disposition to make a second marriage, either in the county set, or in the little town world of Market Dalling, where the Rigbys themselves lived and had their important being.

"Kate—you don't understand," he said at last, and, even as he uttered the words, they seemed to him painfully inadequate. "In fact, you never *did* understand"—there came a sudden touch of passion into his voice, and he got up and walked up and down the room—"how I felt—how for the matter of that I still feel—about Rosaleen. But for the war—but for the getting clear away—I don't know what I should have done! Once, when I was out there in a little out-of-the-way station, I saw an old bill with her name on it, put up, of course, before I met her, when she was touring in South Africa. Well, I can tell you one thing—if we had been back in the days when a soldier could get killed so much more easily than he can now, you would never have seen me again. For days and days I couldn't get her out of my mind—she's never out of my mind now——"

Mrs. Rigby was frightened, almost awed, not so much by the violence of his feeling, as by the outspoken expression of that feeling.

She got up and walked quickly to him.

"Perhaps I understand more than you think," she said in a moved voice, "but now, David, you must turn your back on all that. For good or evil, it's over and done with, and your duty is to your child. I won't say a word against Mary Scanlan,—I know she's been a faithful servant to you,—but wouldn't it be better for Rosy if you had someone who could look after the house, as well as after her? Even you admit that you cannot go on at the Brew House as you've been doing lately. I know you can't feel to anyone else as you felt to—to Rosaleen, but surely it would be best for the child, to say nothing of yourself, to have some kind, nice woman about the place, instead of one who's only a servant after all."

"Of course, it would be better," he said sombrely. "Don't you think I know that? But where am I to find the 'nice, kind woman'? As for the girls I meet, it's out of the question."

As he spoke, he unconsciously glanced round the room in which he and his sister were standing. Mrs. Rigby had not inherited the good taste which had distinguished her Banfield forefathers. The Brew House was full of fine old furniture, furniture which some of the young brewer's "grand" friends envied him; but that which the Rigbys had gradually accumulated had the mean and yet rather pretentious commonness which belonged to the period in which they had married.

"There's one whom you've never thought of, but who often thinks of you," said Mrs. Rigby, her voice sinking to a whisper.

Banfield looked at his sister attentively. His fastidious mind passed in review the various young women who composed the little society of Market Dalling. He regarded them all with indifference, rising in some cases to positive dislike, and since his matrimonial misfortunes he had, as far as was possible, avoided every kind of social gathering held in his native place.

"I don't know whom you mean," he said at last with some discomfiture. "In the old days you were always apt to fancy that the girls were after me, and I can't say that you ever gave them much encouragement,"—he added with a rather clumsy attempt at playfulness.

"The person I have in my mind," persisted Mrs. Rigby, "isn't exactly a girl; she's just what we were talking about—a nice, kind woman—and you never seem to mind meeting her."

"Do you—can you possibly mean——"

"——Matilda Wellow? Yes, of course I do. It's astonishing to me, it's even surprising to Matthew, that you've never noticed how much she likes you. Why, she's the only person in Market Dalling who ever takes any trouble about little Rosy, or who ever gives the child anything; Rosy always calls her Auntie Tiddy."

"Matilda Wellow?" he repeated, honestly bewildered. "Why, of course I like her, and think well of her, but I've never thought of her—and don't believe she's ever thought of me, Kate—in that way!"

"Don't you?" she said drily. "There's none so blind as those who won't see."

Then, prompted by a shrewd instinct, she remained quite silent, and withdrew her anxious gaze from her brother's face.

Only to-day Banfield had received a letter from South Africa which had sorely tempted him to throw up everything and make a home in the country which, perhaps unfortunately for himself, held none of the glamour of the unknown. As a matter of fact, the letter was now in his pocket, and he felt guiltily aware of the angry pain with which his sister would regard the offer, especially if she guessed how tempting was its effect on his imagination.

But during their strange conversation he had realised, as he had never done before, that there were only two ways open to him—either to go away and make a new life, or to attempt some such solution of his troubles as that which his sister had just proposed to him.

So it was that during those moments of tense silence Matilda Wellow assumed in David Banfield's mind the importance of an only alternative. Perhaps the very fact that the young man was so familiar with her personality, while always regarding her as a contemporary of his sister, made it easier for him to come to a sudden decision.

To another important fact—never forgotten for a moment by Mrs. Rigby—namely, that Miss Wellow was the wealthiest spinster in Market Dalling, Banfield gave no thought, and it certainly played no part in his hurried, anxious self-communing.

"I confess," he said at last, "that this is a new idea to me—but that's no reason why it should be a bad idea. And if you really believe that it would be better for Rosy, and that Miss Wellow would not—" he hesitated awkwardly, "think it strange of me, I will do as you advise, Kate. But you must let me take my own time. Perhaps when she's heard what I've got to say, she won't feel about it as you believe she's likely to do. I cannot pretend that I—well, that I—" his lips refused to form the word—to him the infinitely sacred word—of love.

Mrs. Rigby was bewildered, awed into deep joy. No piece of good fortune which could have befallen herself would have given her so acute a feeling—it almost amounted to pain—of passionate relief, and David Banfield, dimly gathering that it was so, felt exceedingly moved. Surely it was worth almost anything in the way of self-sacrifice to have brought such a look to his sister's face?

They both moved more closely to one another and she, so chary of caress, put her arms round his neck.

"I'm quite sure," she spoke with a catch in her voice, "quite, quite sure that you will never regret it! After all, life does get smoothed out, doesn't it? I'll tell you something about myself that I've never told anybody. Before Matthew came along, there was someone else I loved—loved, maybe, just as dearly as you loved Rosaleen."

"I know," said her brother, wincing at the sound of his late wife's name, "you mean Nat Bower?"

"Why, how did you ever guess that?" she asked, surprised.

"Oh! he used to take me walks when I was a kid, and he always talked about you."

Had Mrs. Rigby left the matter there, she would have been a wiser woman, but something prompted her to draw a moral.

"And don't you think I'm glad now?" she cried. "Think of what that poor fellow has become, and what Matthew is now!"

But this was too much for David Banfield.

"I don't think that's fair!" he exclaimed. "What you ought to say is—'Think of what that poor fellow might have become if he had married me!' I don't believe any man could have helped going straight with you, Kate. If I'd been more like you——"

Then, to the young man's relief, his brother-in-law, Matthew Rigby, came into the room, with a smile on his thin lips, a joke on his tongue.

Mrs. Rigby went out into the garden. "Matilda!" she cried. "Tiddy dear, come in! Matt is here. Dinner will be ready in a minute."

But as the two women met, and together walked down the path, the hostess gave her guest no hint of the good fortune which lay in wait for her—indeed, in spite of, or perhaps because of, her moment of softening, she was sharply, almost cruelly, intolerant of Miss Wellow's sentimental references to that ceremony of which they were about to celebrate the twenty-fifth anniversary.

And now the Silver Wedding festivity was drawing to a close.

The dinner, in its old-fashioned way, had been really excellent, for Kate Rigby was a notable housewife; but not even that fact, nor the equally excellent champagne—for Matthew Rigby was too shrewd a man to drink bad wine—had had the effect of brightening the little party, and a certain constraint now sat on the four people who were linked so closely together.

The host, a man of equable temperament, felt faintly uncomfortable; as he looked from one to the other, he told himself that something was wrong.

His brother-in-law was certainly oddly unlike himself, yet surely David Banfield was too sensible, and by this time too well accustomed to his sister's ways, to have taken offence at anything she might have said concerning the well-worn subject of Brew House domestic difficulties. Mrs. Rigby was also unnaturally silent, and during the long course of the meal she uttered none of the sharp pungent sayings with which she generally enlivened each one of her husband's repasts and which, it must be admitted, never to him lost their savour. Last, but not least, Miss Wellow, whose flowered muslin gown was as much too youthful as that of her hostess was too old, seemed more sentimental and more foolish than usual.

Mr. Rigby told himself with much satisfaction that his Kate had certainly worn better than Tiddy Wellow. And yet——? Yet, twenty-five years ago, Tiddy had been such a pretty girl! Soft and round, with dewy brown eyes and pink dimpled cheeks. She still had the appealing, inconsequent manner which, so charming in a girl, is apt to be absurd in a woman—and then she had grown stout! Mr. Rigby liked a woman to have a neat trim figure—his Kate had kept hers—but Tiddy. Alas! Tiddy had not been so fortunate.

So it was that Mr. Rigby paid poor Miss Wellow but little attention, regarding her with a curious mixture of affectionate contempt and respect, the former due to his knowledge of her character, and the latter to his knowledge of her very considerable fortune.

Even to such a man as Matthew Rigby,—that is, to a man whose profession implies the constant hearing of family secrets, and the coming across of strange, almost inconceivable human occurrences,—the melancholy domestic story of David Banfield remained painfully vivid. On him had fallen all the arrangements which had finally resulted in the divorce, and, unlike his wife, he had sometimes doubted the wisdom of what he and she had brought about, for Banfield, left to himself, would never have severed the legal tie between himself and the mother of his child.

Even now, during the course of his Silver Wedding dinner, Matthew Rigby wondered uneasily whether his wife's constrained silence, and his brother-in-law's odd, abstracted manner, meant that any tidings had been received of the woman who had now so completely passed out of their lives. But Mr. Rigby was compelled to bide his time. He knew that whatever explanation there was would be given to him once he and Kate were alone together.

Sure enough, when the two men joined the ladies in the now twilit sitting-room, the hostess lost no time in unceremoniously turning her brother and Miss Wellow out into the garden.

And then, at once, Matthew Rigby realised that something of real importance and moment had indeed occurred. For the first time since the great day when her brother's divorce had become an absolute fact, Mrs. Rigby seemed inclined to be soft and tender in her manner to the man who, she would have been the first to admit, had been to her the most admirable of husbands.

There are certain human beings, men perhaps, more than women, who use those they love as princes of old used their whipping boys, and among these human beings Mrs. Rigby could certainly have claimed a high place. Matthew Rigby was, therefore, the more surprised, even, perhaps, a little relieved, when he noted the unwonted tenderness with which she slipped her arm through his; it couldn't be anything so very bad after all!

"I don't suppose I need tell you, Matt, what has happened—or what is just going to happen—to our David and Tiddy Wellow?" and she nodded her head significantly towards the two figures which were now disappearing into the rustic arbour, which, erected by Mrs. Rigby's father-in-law, some thirty years ago, had always vexed her thrifty soul as an extravagant and useless addition to her garden; just now, however, she would have admitted that even arbours have their uses.

"Phew———!" exclaimed Matthew Rigby, and had it not been for the presence of his wife, he would certainly have sworn some decorous form of oath to express his extreme surprise. His pause prolonged itself, and then, with a certain effort, he exclaimed: "You're an even cleverer woman than I took you for, Kate, and that's saying a good deal!"

Mrs. Rigby turned and looked at him steadily. Their heads were almost on a level, but even she could guess nothing from his expression. It was his tone, rather, that jarred on her very true contentment.

"Surely you think it's the best thing that could happen to him?" she asked, a note of wistful anxiety in her voice. "Why, you and I have talked it over dozens of times!"

"I've heard *you* say that you thought Matilda Wellow was the very woman for him, time and again, but—but I don't think, Kate, you ever heard *me* say so. Still, I daresay it's all right; you generally know best,"—and the husband spoke with less irony than might have been expected. Twenty-five years of married life had taught him that, on the whole, his wife generally did know best.

"And surely you think so, too?" and she pressed more closely to him, "surely, Matt, you don't doubt that Matilda Wellow will make him a good wife, and be kind to the child?"

"Of course, I've no doubt about that," he answered reassuringly. "But still, she's not exactly the woman I'd have chosen for myself, and, after all, David was very fond of that queer, cold little hussy."

Mrs. Rigby was given no time for a reply, for her brother and Miss Wellow were coming slowly towards the house. She turned up the gas with a quick movement, and when they approached the window a glance at her future sister-in-law's face was enough. She saw that David had spoken, but she also saw that he had had the power—and unconsciously her respect for her brother grew—to stifle in his companion the mingled emotions his offer of marriage had called forth.

Not till the long dull evening was over, not till Banfield and Miss Wellow were actually bidding the Rigbys good-night, did the young man say the word which let loose Matilda's incoherent words of pathetic joy, of rather absurd amazement, at the good fortune which had befallen her.

Mrs. Rigby bustled out the two men into the hall.

"Matilda! Don't be silly!" she commanded.

But her words had no effect.

"It's just a dream—" gasped Miss Wellow, "just a dream come true! I never thought, Kate, to be so happy—and dear little Rosy, too——"

The other woman checked her harshly.

"Don't be a fool, Tiddy!" she said in a low, stern voice; "if my brother were a different kind of man he'd make you remember this to your dying day. You're lowering yourself—and you're not raising him. Don't go behaving like a pullet that's just laid her first egg!"

Then, seeing the other's face redden into a painful blush, "There, there, I shouldn't have said that, I know. But I can't bear to see a woman cheapen herself to a man!"

Banfield and his new betrothed walked arm in arm through the now sleeping town to the garden gate of the old Georgian house where Miss Wellow had now lived for some five years in solitary spinster state, and where her forefathers had led lives of agreeable, if monotonous, respectability for over a hundred years.

When they reached the gate, each hesitated a moment. Miss Wellow longed to ask him in, but like most maiden ladies possessed of means, she had a tyrant, a Cerberus in the shape of a faithful servant who would now be sitting up waiting sulkily for her mistress's return. Banfield was awkwardly debating with himself whether Matilda expected him to kiss her; on the whole he thought—he hoped—not.

But he was spared the onus of decision concerning this delicate point; for suddenly he felt himself drawn on one side, and there, in the deep shadow of the wall, his companion threw her arms about him, murmuring, with a catch in her voice, "I know you don't love me yet, but—but—David, I'll *make* you love me," and the face turned up to his in the half darkness was full of eager yearning.

Feeling a traitor—to himself, to Rosaleen, above all, to the poor soul now leaning on his breast—Banfield bent and kissed her; then he turned on his heel, leaving her to make her way as best she could up the trim path leading to her front door.

Hardly aware of what he was doing, he walked away quickly, taking the opposite direction to that of the quiet lane of houses which would have led him straight home. Instead he struck out, instinctively, towards the flat open country, for he had a fierce, unreasoning desire to be alone—far away from all humankind. As he strode along, his eyes having become so fully accustomed to the dim light that he could see every detail of the white-rutted road gleaming between low hedges, Banfield's feeling of bewilderment, even of horror, grew and grew, making him feel physically cold in the warm, scented night.

For the first time there swept over him that awful sense of unavailing repentance for the word said which might so well have been left unsaid, which most human beings are fated to feel at some time of their lives.

Not even over his divorce had he felt so desperate a passion of revolt, for that act, or so he had believed, was forced on him by Rosaleen herself. But to-night he realised that before doing what he had just done he had been free—free to remain free—and he now saw with a sense of impotent anger how deliberately he had given himself into slavery.

As he strode along, eager to escape from the material surroundings of his surrender, Banfield remembered each word of his talk with his sister, and so remembering, he was amazed at his own weak folly.

What were the trifling troubles connected with his Irish servant, Mary Scanlan, compared to those which lay before him?—to the awful knowledge that he was now the prisoner—henceforth the body and soul prisoner—of Matilda Wellow? How sluggish had been his imagination when he had thought of the woman, whose tears had but just now scalded his lips, as of a kind, unobtrusive lady housekeeper! He was now aware that there was another Matilda Wellow, of whom till to-night he had been ignorant, and it was this stranger who was demanding as a right, and indeed had the right to demand, that tenderness and devotion which he knew himself incapable of bestowing on any woman except on the elusive, cold-natured woman who had been his wife.

And then a strange thing happened to David Banfield.

The near image of Matilda Wellow faded, giving place to the distant, and yet in a spiritual and even physical sense poignantly present, personality of Rosaleen.

As far as was possible, Banfield till to-night had banished his wife's image from his emotional memory. But what he had just done—that is, his own lack of constancy—had the odd effect of making him feel lowered to the level to which those about him regarded Rosaleen as fallen. He told himself that now he and Rosaleen were quits—and deliberately he yielded to the cruel luxury of recollection.

His mind travelled back to the early days of their acquaintance, to the pretence at a "friendship" which on his side had so soon become overwhelming passion. Then had come his formal offer of marriage, and for a long time she had played with him, saying neither yes nor no. Then for a while he had flung everything to the winds in order to be with her—on any terms. He remembered with a pang of pain the trifling reasons which at last made her quite suddenly consent to become his wife. A quarrel with the manager of the concert company to which she then belonged, followed by a bad notice in the local paper of the town to which he, David Banfield, undeterred by more than one half-laughing refusal, had come to make what he intended should be a final offer—these, it seemed, had brought Rosaleen to the point of decision.

Even now, Banfield never heard the name of that little Sussex town without a leap of the heart, for it was there that had taken place their marriage, the quietest and least adorned of weddings, celebrated in a small, bare Roman Catholic chapel, the incumbent of which, a wise old man, had spoken to Banfield very seriously, asking him to give the young Irishwoman more time for thought, and impressing upon him the gravity of the promises which he, a Protestant, had consented to make concerning their future married life.

With regard to the latter, Banfield had been scrupulously honourable, going, indeed, out of his way to remind Rosaleen of her religious obligations, and at the time of the divorce acting, in the matter of their child's future education, according to the spirit rather than the letter of his promise....

With bent head and eyes fixed on the white road, David Banfield insensibly slackened his steps while his mind concerned itself with the five years he and Rosaleen had spent together at Market Dalling. They had been years of secret drama, on his part of almost wordless struggle for some kind of response to the passion which her mysterious aloofness—to so many men the greater part of a woman's attraction—evoked and kept alive in him.

He now remembered how during these years there had been minor causes of disagreement, trifling matters—or so he had considered them—to which Rosaleen attached far more importance than he had done.

The constant criticism and interference of his half-sister, the dislike and jealousy of those town folk who regarded themselves as having a right to the close friendship and intimacy of David Banfield's young wife, these were the things—forming such unimportant asides to the course of that hidden struggle—which Rosaleen had brought forward when begging her husband, with passionate energy, to allow her to go back to her profession.

But to-night, the grey fear with which he now regarded his own future life at Market Dalling brought to David Banfield a sudden understanding of what Rosaleen had felt, caged, as he had caged her, in the little town to which he was now reluctantly turning his laggard steps, and which had been, till so few years ago, the centre of his universe.

He told himself that had he had the courage, had he been possessed of the necessary imagination, to make another life for himself and for her, none of this need have happened.

But why torture himself uselessly? He and Rosaleen had now drifted as far apart as a man and a woman can drift. What he had done to-night was in its way as irrevocable as what she on her side had done—nay more, the very fact that he had Matilda Wellow so completely at his mercy made Banfield feel, as a less simple-hearted, generous-minded man would never have felt, how impossible it was for him to draw back....

While returning to what had now become his place of bondage, David Banfield made a determined effort to dam the mental floodgates through which had run so strange a stream of violent revolt and emotion, and he was so far rewarded that almost at once something occurred which had the effect of bracing him up, of hardening him in his determination to do what he believed to be right.

As he walked down the silent, shuttered High Street at the end of which stood the Brew House, he saw that his hall light had not been extinguished;

and as he opened the front door, he was confronted with the spare form and the gaunt, though not ill-visaged countenance of Mary Scanlan, the elderly Irishwoman who had for so long waged triumphant battle with her master's sister, Mrs. Rigby. Utterly different as the two women were, they yet, as Banfield sometimes secretly told himself, not without a certain sore amusement, had strong points of resemblance the one with the other.

Impelled by some obscure instinct that thus was he certain to be strengthened in the course of action to which he had just pledged himself, Banfield invited the woman into the dining-room, which had been, since his first wife's departure, used by him as living and eating room in one.

Very deliberately he lit the gas, and then turned and faced his housekeeper. "I think it right that you should be among the first to know," he said, "that I am going to be married again—to Miss Wellow."

There was a moment's pause. Banfield expected either a word of sullen acquiescence or an outburst of anger; he had known Mary Scanlan in both moods, but now she surprised him by assuming a very disconcerting attitude.

"If that's the case," she said slowly, twisting and untwisting a corner of the black apron that she was wearing, "I will be getting ready little Rosy's clothes, for you will be sending her to the convent rather sooner, I reckon, than you meant to do. I make no doubt the nuns will let me stay there for a week or two till the child gets accustomed to the place—that is, if you have no objection, Mr. Banfield?"

Banfield looked at the woman in some perplexity.

"But I've no thought of sending Rosy to school yet!" he exclaimed—then added: "Of course, I mean to keep my promise to her mother, but—but the child's a little thing yet—too young to go to school."

Mary Scanlan was the only woman to whom Banfield ever spoke of his wife, and Mrs. Rigby would have been amazed indeed had she known how often these allusions and semi-allusions were made, for to Kate, much as he trusted and respected his sister, Banfield had never till that day bared his heart.

"I am going to ask you," he went on, "to stay in my service, simply to look after the child. I know well, Mary, how devoted you are to my little girl, and how good you've been to her. When Miss Wellow has become—" he hesitated awkwardly, and then with a certain effort, uttered the words "my wife—she will, of course, take charge of the house, and I suppose she will bring her own servants with her. I shall no longer have any need for a housekeeper—but I know she will be only too glad if you will stay on with Rosy."

"I don't think I can do that, sir."

Banfield moved uneasily. Mary Scanlan almost invariably called him "Mr. Banfield"; it was one of the woman's many Irish idiosyncrasies which irritated his sister.

"I don't think I can stay on here, sir," repeated Mary Scanlan in a low, hesitating voice. "I don't hold with a man, a gentleman I mean, having two wives. I can't say a word of excuse for my poor Miss Rosaleen—I beg your pardon, sir, I mean Mrs. Banfield. I know she behaved very wickedly and strangely, but still you see, Mr. Banfield, to my thinking and according to my holy religion, she's the woman who owns you, sir, and no one else can ever take her place."

"I know, I know," he said hastily. "But Mary, why don't you consult your priest? If you explain the circumstances to him, he may take a different view of the matter to what you do."

"No, that he wouldn't!" exclaimed Mary Scanlan, with a touch of her old passionate temper, "and if he did, I shouldn't be said by him!"

She hesitated, and then in a low tone asked the strange question, made the amazing suggestion, "I suppose you wouldn't be after seeing Miss Rosaleen, Mr. Banfield? Not if I gave you her address?"

Banfield made a nervous movement of recoil.

"Mary," he said sternly, "you forget yourself!" and turning, left her in possession of the room.

How describe the days that followed?—short days full of intense joy and looking forward to Matilda Wellow, long days filled with perplexed misgiving and self-reproach to David Banfield.

Men and women of British birth generally prefer to conduct their courtships in the way that best suits themselves, but those whom Mrs. Rigby collectively dubbed as "foreigners" have long ago realised the advantage of having so important an episode of human life as that of betrothal "stage-managed" by someone more experienced in such matters than the two most interested.

Mrs. Rigby had no kind of sympathy with foreign fashion, and in theory thoroughly disapproved of the way in which the French, for instance, arrange their matrimonial affairs. But this engagement of her brother David

Banfield and of Matilda Wellow was one of the supreme exceptions which prove a rule, and so she stage-managed every entrance, every exit, and, to pursue the analogy to its bitter end, every bit of "business" connected with the affair.

Her stern eyes, her rough tongue, kept the bride-elect in order, but her watchful fear lest Matilda should get on David's nerves before she became securely bound to him for ever had one curious effect; it made Banfield sorry for his betrothed, and caused him to feel more kindly to her than he would otherwise have done.

Then he was touched and surprised by Matilda's great loyalty to himself; he soon discovered that, far from discussing him with his sister, she often irritated the latter by her assumption that already she, Matilda, and he, David, had a joint life in which Kate Rigby played no part. This angered Mrs. Rigby keenly, and it is a pathetic fact that the only tears Matilda Wellow shed during the course of her engagement were caused by the woman who was her oldest friend, and to whom she was dimly aware that she owed her good-fortune.

Blinded by that most blinding of master passions, jealousy, Mrs. Rigby actually came to believe that her brother was now attached, in a far truer sense than he had been to Rosaleen, to the fond, foolish woman who was so soon to become his wife.

"He's getting quite silly about her," she observed angrily to her husband; "he goes up there every evening, however busy he may be, or however much I may want to have him here. And now he says he won't go to that good London tailor for his wedding clothes! It's clear he doesn't want to leave Tiddy—even for three days!"

But Mr. Rigby, as was his prudent wont when he disagreed with his wife, only looked at her, and thoughtfully wagged his head.

"Why don't you say something?" she asked crossly.

"Why should David go to London?" observed Mr. Rigby mildly. "He's a personable fellow; any tailor could fit David. If I were you, Kate, I'd let him be." But Kate, to her lasting sorrow, did not let David be.

Both her husband and even Matilda Wellow herself could have told Mrs. Rigby that it was in London that her brother had spent his honeymoon with his wife; but though she had been made vividly aware of the circumstance—for it was from there that the news of his hasty marriage had reached her—that fact would not have seemed to her any reason why David should not now do the right and proper thing by his second bride.

Thus it was owing to Mrs. Rigby that Matilda was at last roused to a sense of what was due to herself. Banfield, with some discomfiture, discovered that Miss Wellow would take it ill of him not to pay her the compliment of going to the London tailor for his wedding clothes—"and then," had observed his sister briskly, "you'll be able to bring Tiddy back something handsome in the way of jewellery; for that's a thing you owe not only to her, David, but also to yourself."

II

David Banfield, just arrived in London, stood in an hotel bedroom overlooking the trees in Lincoln's Inn Fields.

Staring out at the leafy screen, which seemed to him so lacking in country freshness, there came to his mind poignant memories of a very different room and a very different outlook not half a mile away from where he stood, for he and Rosaleen had spent the first days of their married life in one of those vast hotels which, overlooking the Embankment and the river, are filled with light and air, as well as instinct with a certain material luxury which had pleased his young wife's taste more than his own.

With a quick movement he pushed up the old-fashioned guillotine window as far as it would go, and leaned out dangerously far; then he drew back sharply, feeling, as he now often felt when he was alone, that he was living through an unreal, a nightmare stage of his life, one which was bound to come sooner or later to an abrupt end, but which now must be lived through....

With unseeing eyes and unthinking mind he walked across to the shadowed corner where had been placed his portmanteau. Slowly, indifferently, he turned the key in the lock and raised the lid,—then quickened into alert, painful attention.

Lying on the top of its neatly folded contents was an envelope so placed that it could not but attract his attention, and on it was written—in the sprawling, unformed handwriting which was, perhaps, the only marked betrayal of Mary Scanlan's early lack of education—the one word "Important."

At once there leapt into Banfield's mind the certain knowledge of what the envelope contained. If he opened it, there most surely would he find his wife Rosaleen's address. It was this, then, that the Irishwoman had in her thoughts when she had asked him the unseemly question to which he had given so short and stern an answer.

But Mary Scanlan had not understood the type of man with whom she had to deal.

As he stood there, longing with a terrible longing to verify his belief, telling himself, with a leap of the heart, that, if he were not mistaken, then Rosaleen must be living alone, for if this had not been so the old servant would never have thought of trying to bring them together again—the claims of others, especially those of the woman from whom he had only parted that morning, became paramount. He told himself that, from the point of view of those who loved him, and whom he respected, it was his duty to destroy unopened the envelope lying before him.

Banfield turned away, and once more walked across to the window; and then his agitation suddenly became puerile in his eyes.

What the Irishwoman had regarded as important when packing his bag might well be a trifling matter, something wanted, maybe, for the child. The uncertainty seemed to steady his conscience; *he felt that he must know.*

Bending down, he took up the envelope; the flap was open, and out of it there slipped into his hand a shabby little card on which was printed:

MISS ROSALEEN TARA (The Colleen Bawn),18, Abbey Street,Westminster, S. W.

There followed for David Banfield three days of agonising struggle and temptation. All the feelings and instincts he had battened down, put determinedly from him for so long, sprang into life. Now that he knew where to find her, he became possessed by a deep, unreasoning longing to see Rosaleen once more—even if a meeting could only result in pain for him, in shame for her.

On the second day of his stay in London, he offered conscience a salve in the form of a fine ruby ring, which was despatched to Miss Wellow in lieu of the letter which he knew only too well she must be anxiously awaiting.

Had Banfield been a stronger man he would have left London. But that, or so he told himself, there was no need to do; and as the hours dragged on, bringing him closer to the moment which must see his return to Market Dalling—to Matilda Wellow—the fact that he and Rosaleen were in a material sense so near to one another began to affect his imagination in strangest and most poignant fashion.

Walking aimlessly along the hot airless streets of London in July, he found himself ever furtively seeking her.... Such chance meetings are not impossible; they happen every day. Why should such a thing not come to him as well as to another?

And so in the summer twilight, not once but many times, some woman's form—slender, graceful, light-footed as was Rosaleen's—would create for a moment the illusion that she was there, close to him, would bring the wild hope that in a moment his hungry heart would be satisfied, his conscience cheated. And then the woman in whom he had seen for a moment his poor lost love, would turn her head—and Banfield, cast down but undismayed, would again pursue his eager, aimless search.

On the last evening of his stay in London, this obsession became so intense that Banfield saw Rosaleen in every woman's shape that passed him by. He grew afraid; and after an hour spent in the peopled streets, he told himself that that way madness lay.

With eyes fixed on the dusty pavements, he made his way back to his hotel, and sitting down he wrote a letter—a kind, cheerful letter—to Matilda Wellow, telling her that he would be with her the next afternoon at five o'clock. And then, for the first time since he had known that Rosaleen was in London, his sleep was restful and unbroken. But in the early morning he dreamed a curious dream; Rosaleen, the beloved, the longed-for woman, was again with him,—elusive, mysterious, teasing as she had ever been,—and Banfield, waking in the early dawn, felt tears of joy standing on his face.

When he got up in the morning, and faced the day which was to see him go back to Market Dalling, he felt as must feel a man who sees stretching before him a lifelong period of servitude; but with that feeling came the gloomy belief that he had conquered the temptation that had so beset him, and this being so, he argued that he had at least a right to see the place where Rosaleen now lived.

Having come to this specious understanding with himself, Banfield felt his heart lighten. He told himself that he would wait till he was within some two hours of the time when he knew he must leave London, and, having so decided, he checked his impatience by various devices, packing his portmanteau, paying his bill, doing first one thing and then another, till the moment came for him to start walking along the Embankment to Westminster.

When at last he reached the broad, wind-swept space out of which he had been told turned Abbey Street, quietest and most sequestered of urban backwaters, he lingered for awhile, suddenly filled with an obscure fear of that for which he had so longed—a chance meeting with his wife.

After a few moments of indecision, he started walking slowly down the middle of the street, his footfalls echoing on the cobblestones.

Banfield looked about him curiously. To the right stretched the rough grey wall of London's oldest garden, framing a green oasis opposite the row of small eighteenth-century houses which stood on the other side of the street. They were quaint, shabby little dwellings, and against more than one fanlight was displayed a card bearing the word "Lodgings."

When Banfield came opposite No. 18, he stopped and looked up at the windows with beating heart and the colour rushed into his face, flooding it under the sunburn; following a sudden, an irresistible impulse, he stepped up on to the pavement, and with a nervous movement pulled the bell.

Then followed what seemed to him a long wait on the doorstep, but at last a thin, fretful woman came to the door and enquired his business.

"Does Miss Rosaleen Tara live here? Can I see her?"

"Yes, she lives 'ere right enough,"—the woman spoke with weary indifference,—"come this way."

Banfield paused; he had never thought the access to Rosaleen would be so simple, and he was bewildered by the ease with which this, to him so momentous a step, had been compassed.

He followed the woman up the narrow, wainscoted staircase to a tiny landing. "Stop," he said almost inaudibly, "I must tell you what to say—you must not show me straight in to her, like this."

But even as he spoke, there was another tinkle of the bell, and the woman began running heavily down the little staircase, leaving him standing in front of the door.

He knocked, but there came no answer, and at last he turned the handle, and walked into the room. It was empty of human presence, and yet his wife had stamped something of herself on the shabbily furnished sitting-room. Certain dainty trifles which he had known as hers were there, and before him, on the piano, was a music-case which he himself had given her.

The sight of this, his own gift, affected Banfield oddly, giving him a feeling that he had a right to be there. After a moment's hesitation, he walked over to the window, and looked out into the old Abbey garden. There he would wait patiently—for hours if need be—till Rosaleen came in.

Then, quite suddenly, there fell on his ear the voice which he had so often heard in dreams, and which he had of late so passionately longed to hear. He turned sharply round, and noticed for the first time that the door of the inner room was ajar. It was from thence that the light, indifferent tones floated impalpably towards him.

"Ah! but it's kind of you, doctor, to come so soon after Miss Lonsdale asked you to see me! I've only just come in, but I won't be a moment—I didn't expect you yet. Miss Lonsdale will be in long before you leave, I hope; she's almost as anxious about my voice as I am—and the faith she has in you, why, it's something wonderful!"

To Banfield, the words recalled, not Rosaleen his wife, but Rosaleen the girl, the dear bewitching stranger he had first known and wooed, though never won. Unconsciously he visualised the speaker; he seemed to see the quick, bird-like movements with which she was taking off her hat and smoothing her hair before the glass. He even saw her smiling—smiling as she used to smile at him in the very early days of their acquaintance.

He knew that he ought to cry out—tell her that it was he, her husband, David Banfield, who was there, and not the stranger whom she had apparently been expecting; but though he opened his lips, no word would come.

At last the door swung open quickly, and for a moment Banfield saw her face, lit up by that touch of wholly innocent coquetry of which your pretty Irishwoman seems to have the secret.

Then, as suddenly she realised the identity of the tall man standing between her and the window, a peculiar—to Banfield a very terrible—change of expression stiffened Rosaleen's face into watchful fear and attention.

"What is it?" she asked. "Tell me quickly, David! Is Rosy ill, or—or dead?"

"Rosy?" he stammered. "She's all right. I heard this morning——"

"—And I yesterday," she breathed quickly. Then she sat down, and Banfield let his eyes rest on her with a painful, yearning scrutiny.

He had thought to find her altered, coarsened by the experience he believed her to have gone through, but she had the same look of delicate, rather frigid refinement, which had first attracted him. He noted the perfection of her delicate profile, the determined, well-shaped mouth,—then saw with a pang that there were a few threads of white in the dark curly hair which, with her bright blue eyes, had always been Rosaleen's principal beauties; and yet she looked scarcely older than on the day he had last seen her—that on which he had accompanied her with a heavy heart to the station at Market Dalling to see her off to London.

Now, looking at her, it stabbed him to remember how even then she had shown an almost childish joy in leaving him. She had put her arms round his neck and kissed him in sign of gratitude. "It's kind of you to let me go, Dave!" she had whispered. He had often thought of those last words, the last he had heard her speak. Now he again remembered them. Alas! alas! why had he let her go?

She sat, looking away from him, her eyes fixed on the empty grate.

"You frightened me," she said plaintively. "Why did you come here, David, and frighten me like this? Why have you come here at all after—after what you did to me?"

"What I did to you?" he stammered confusedly, and there came over him the shamed fear that she had already heard of his coming marriage with Matilda Wellow.

"Yes, what you did to me—the documents you sent me—divorce papers they're called——" He felt, rather than saw, that his wife's eyes were filling, brimming over with indignant tears. "We don't have those things at home—in Ireland, I mean. And then reading out my letter—the mad letter I sent you—before a lot of men!"

Rosaleen had always possessed the wifely art of being able to make David Banfield feel himself in the wrong, and now, on hearing her last words, the man before her told himself with a pang that he had indeed acted in an unkind, even an unmanly, fashion to the fragile-looking woman who sat with her face averted from him.

"I thought—of course I thought"—he plucked up courage as he spoke—"that you wanted to be free. You said you hoped I should forget you."

"—And so I did," she said quickly, "I did wish to be free—not so much from you, as from the miserable, the stiflingly dull life you made me lead at Market Dalling. That's why I wrote that foolish—that wicked letter. I thought it would make you leave me alone. But, David," she made a restless movement, "I didn't understand. However, I've been well punished."

There was a short, strained silence. Then Rosaleen got up.

"I'm afraid I can't ask you to stay on much longer," she began nervously, "for I'm expecting a doctor who was very kind to me once when I was ill before. He's a friend of Carrie Lonsdale—you remember her, David? The truth is, my voice has given out, and I've been trying to give lessons, but Carrie thinks he will be able to make it come back again soon."

"And what will you do," asked Banfield in a very low voice, "if he fails?"

She turned and looked up at him, her eyes meeting his in direct challenge.

"Whatever I do," she said proudly, "you need not fear that I shall come to you for any help."

And then David Banfield felt shaken, overwhelmed by a fierce spasm of violent, primitive jealousy. The name of the other man had never been forthcoming; Rosaleen's letter had sufficed to win the undefended suit.

"I suppose," he said brutally, "that you can always depend on getting help from your lover?"

Rosaleen's eyes dropped, her face flushed darkly as she saw the change which came over her husband's face and as there came into his voice accents she had never heard there.

She sprang up. "How dare you insult me? You have no right to say such a thing to me! I am free to do exactly what I like and to go to whom I choose—you yourself made me free!"

But a very different man from the man she had believed David Banfield to be now stood before her.

Of the words she had said, the last alone remained with him. Free? Nay, nay, Rosaleen was in no sense free; his whole nature rose up and protested against such a statement. There could be no question of choice, for she belonged to him, only to him, solely to him, and that even if she had in a moment of aberration, of madness—his mind refused to follow the thought to its logical conclusion—not even in the most secret recess of his imagination had Banfield ever consented to dwell on what he believed had been. Not till the last few moments had he seen the torturing vision which almost always haunts the man who has been betrayed by a beloved woman.

He came yet closer, and put his hand on her shoulder.

"Rosaleen," he said hoarsely, "you don't understand. You want to know why I came here to-day? Well, I came to say that I am thinking of leaving Market Dalling. I came to ask you if you are willing to come back to me—to make a fresh start. You said just now that it was Market Dalling and our life there that you hated—not me. I've had a very good offer to go to South Africa, to Durban, and settle there. There's even a house waiting for us, and a convent school for Rosy. But whether I go or not depends on you, Rosaleen. If you are willing to come with us, we'll all go together—if not, I mean to stay at Market Dalling."

Rosaleen remained quite still. She made no effort to move away from his touch.

"Did you really come to ask me to do that, David, and that although you think so ill of me?" There was a wondering doubt, a softer, kindlier note, than Banfield had ever heard in his wife's voice.

He set his teeth and lied.

"Yes," he said, "that is why I came. Mary Scanlan gave me your address."

"Poor old Mary!" she exclaimed. "I suppose everyone at Market Dalling thinks I'm a bad woman? Your sister, of course, always hoped that I was a bad woman?"

She looked at him as if half expecting him to make some kind of denial. But he remained silent. What answer, what denial could he make? Of course, everyone at Market Dalling thought Rosaleen a bad woman. For the matter of that, none of them had ever thought well of her, not even his own people, not even his sister and her husband had made any attempt to understand her.

Rosaleen's imprudent question made yet another matter, one which Banfield had succeeded for a few moments in completely forgetting, become once more very present to him. With a feeling of terrible self-reproach there rose before him the helpless figure of Matilda Wellow.

"It's not only you," he said slowly, "but I myself who need to make a fresh start. I haven't so much right to blame you as you, Rosaleen, perhaps think—for I myself did a very wrong, a wicked thing——"

She slipped away from under his hand and got up, facing him.

"It's absurd for you to say that," she exclaimed petulantly, "why, you couldn't do anything wicked, David, if you tried! For the matter of that, I never could see—I never have seen—why people are—why people make——" she seemed to be seeking for a word, a phrase; and it was in a whisper that she added the words, "beasts of themselves."

Banfield stared at her, not understanding; for the moment he was too absorbed in his own feelings, in his own remorse, to take much heed of what she was saying.

"Well?" he asked, "well, Rosaleen, shall we both forgive each other—and make a fresh beginning?"

"Yes," she whispered, hanging her head as might have done a naughty child. With a gesture of surrender, she held out her hands. "I'm ashamed of what I did, David—and I'll try to be a better wife to you than I've been up to now."

Poor Banfield! As he took her in his arms his heart beat with suffocating joy; almost any other man would have felt her words, her implied prayer for forgiveness, curiously inadequate.

She looked at him with a peculiar, earnest look, as if trying to make up her mind to a certain course, and then, with a quick movement, she shook herself free and disappeared into the back room.

He heard the sound of a drawer opening, the fumbling of a key. A moment later she came back and thrust a small packet into his hand.

"There," she said, "open that, read what's inside, and then we'll burn it. Thank God, Rosy will never know now the shame you put on her mother. I've often thought how you would feel reading it, if I—died—before—you did!" and each word was punctuated by an angry sob.

The little packet which Rosaleen had placed in Banfield's hand was tied with blue ribbon, and on it was written: "In case of my death, to be forwarded to Mr. Banfield, The Brew House, Market Dalling."

It was Rosaleen's fingers which untied the knotted ribbon and which showed him, laid amid her little store of jewellery,—he had noticed that she still wore her wedding ring,—a sheet of notepaper on which was an attestation, sworn before a Commissioner of Oaths, that the letter which she had written to him, the confession which had sufficed to procure him his divorce, had been—false.

"But why?" he stammered. "Rosaleen—why?"

"Because I hated the life you made me lead at Market Dalling! I hate Market Dalling and the hateful people who live there! You wouldn't even let me play or sing on Sunday. And then, your sister Kate! She never gave me a kind word or look! D'you think that was pleasant?" she asked fiercely,—then more gently she added, "But I'm ashamed, I've always been ashamed of that letter, and I'd no idea, Dave, that it would make you do what it did."

The door behind them opened. Rosaleen turned around; she brushed the angry tears from her cheeks; there came over her tremulous mouth a charming, rather shy smile.

"Doctor," she said quietly, "you've just come in time to see my husband. David, this is Dr. Bendall, who was so kind to me when I was ill."

Banfield held out his hand....

III

It was the late afternoon of the same day, and Mrs. Rigby was sitting as she had sat on her silver wedding day, close to the window of her sitting-room, her busy hands engaged now, as then, in mending house-linen. Now, as then also, she was expecting her brother and Matilda Wellow to dinner, for before Banfield left for London it had been arranged that he and his betrothed should spend that evening with the Rigbys.

Mrs. Rigby allowed the work she was holding to fall on her lap. She looked into her garden with a preoccupied air. The month which had elapsed since her silver wedding day had brought with it great changes in her life, and what she saw before her seemed, in a sense, symbolic of those changes, for in spite of her careful watering and constant attention, the flower-beds, and above all the beautiful herbaceous borders of which she was so proud, were beginning to look parched and withered.

To-night more than ever Mrs. Rigby realised that the marriage of David and Matilda would alter her own life, and that not for the better. Why, in old days David would of course have come in to see his sister on his way from the station, and that even in the now forgotten time when Rosaleen was mistress of the Brew House. To-day her brother had evidently gone straight to Matilda Wellow....

But Mrs. Rigby reminded herself that, taken as a whole, her garden was incomparably fresher and greener than were those of her neighbours on either side; and as to David and Tiddy, she now told herself, almost speaking the words aloud in her anxiety to make them true, that she was pleased—very pleased—with the way everything was going on.

Thus she was glad that the rather absurd secrecy, so insisted on by her brother, would come to an end to-morrow. Of course a few old friends had been told in confidence of the engagement—but considering that this was so, the secret had been very well kept. It was not as if David were a real widower; Mrs. Rigby could not help hoping that he would be spared some of the silly remarks, the foolish congratulations, which fall to the ordinary engaged man. It must be bad enough for him, so the sister told herself, to put up with Tiddy's sentimental raptures. Still, it was a comfort to know that Matilda Wellow was well aware that she was in luck's way! How Tiddy studied David in everything—any other man would have been spoilt!

For the first time, a smile, not a very kind smile, came over Mrs. Rigby's shrewd, rather hard face.

During the last month, Matilda had actually given up eating potatoes and butter, because some fool had told her that in that way she might hope to regain the youthful slenderness of her figure! As for David, his betrothed's little attentions evidently touched him, and no one could say that he was not an attentive lover. Think of the ring he had sent Tiddy, the ruby ring which had arrived yesterday morning, and which must have cost—so Matt, who was learned in such things, declared—not a penny less than £50!

The exact date of the wedding would probably be fixed to-night, for it had been arranged that the marriage was to follow very soon after the announcement of the engagement. There was no reason for delay. Mrs.

Rigby had herself chosen the 3rd of August as the best date, and she had little doubt that she would be able to persuade Dave and Tiddy that no other day would suit them so well.

Suddenly her quick ears caught the sound of footsteps treading down the path to the left, a path hidden from the place where she was now sitting, and a slight frown came over her face. Mrs. Rigby liked her husband to come straight in to her from the office; but lately, he had taken to the tiresome habit of going out by the back way, into the garden, and then suddenly popping round on her.

She looked out expectantly, but the sound of footsteps died away. It must have been one of the maids going down to the extreme end of the garden in search of some kitchen stuff.

Mrs. Rigby again took up her work and began sewing diligently. Yes, the marriage should take place quite quietly on the 3rd of August. Everything was ready—in fact, there was nothing left to wait for. Even Tiddy's wedding gown and headgear had come home.

David had showed himself oddly interested in this wholly feminine question of his bride's attire.

He had actually been to the trouble of choosing the material of which Tiddy's wedding gown was to be made; a white and grey stripe, a thin, gauzy stuff not nearly substantial enough—or so Mrs. Rigby had thought— for the purpose to which it was destined. And then he had persuaded Matilda to go to a new dressmaker, a Frenchwoman who had been lady's maid to one of his grand county acquaintances, and who had just set up for herself in Market Dalling. More wonderful still, David had made a rough drawing from some old picture that had taken his fancy of the hat he desired Matilda to wear on her wedding day! It was a white hat trimmed with long grey feathers, quite unlike Tiddy's usual style....

Suddenly looking up, Mrs. Rigby felt a thrill of something like superstitious fear, for there, making her way round the corner from the summer-house, came, walking very slowly, a woman at once like and unlike Matilda Wellow, clad in a silvery-looking gown and wearing a white hat trimmed with long grey feathers.

As the figure advanced down the path, it took unmistakable shape and substance; here, without a doubt, was Matilda wearing what were to be her wedding garments, and, as Mrs. Rigby suddenly became aware, a Matilda quite unlike her usual homely self!

Who would have thought that simply leaving off potatoes and butter for a month would have made such a change! Or was that change due to the art of the French dressmaker? The silvery-flounced skirt fell in graceful, billowy folds to the ground, for Miss Wellow was not even holding up her gown, as a more sensible woman would have done. The muslin kerchief edged with real lace, outlined the wearer's still pretty shoulders, and the hat—well, the hat was certainly becoming, especially now that Tiddy's cheeks were flushed—as well they might be, considering what a fool the woman was making of herself!

Mrs. Rigby felt rather cross at having been so startled; she got up, and walked out to meet her guest, determined not to be drawn into any praise of the becoming hat and gown.

"I hope David won't keep us waiting long," she said tartly. "I suppose he thought that he must put on his dress suit," and her expression showed clearly that in the matter of overdressing there was not much to choose between her brother and the woman who was to become his wife.

"David will not be here to-night, Kate. He came, but he has gone away again—back to London."

Miss Wellow spoke in a low, collected voice, and certain little irritating mannerisms with which she usually punctuated her words were absent. Perhaps it was the quiet, expressionless way in which she made her surprising statement that caused Mrs. Rigby, as she afterwards averred to her husband, at once to feel that something was wrong.

"Gone back to London?" the sister repeated. "Why, whatever has he done that for? What business took him back to London, to-day?" and she looked searchingly at the other's flushed face.

"Kate," said Miss Wellow, again speaking in the soft, emotionless voice which was so unlike her own, "I have got to tell you something which I fear will upset you—and make you very angry with poor David. Kate—he has gone back to Rosaleen."

Mrs. Rigby withdrew her eyes quickly from Matilda Wellow's face. She did not then realise that the words which had just been spoken would for ever spoil to her this fragrant, familiar corner of her garden. All she felt now was a fierce, instinctive wish to get under shelter,—to hear whatever shameful thing had to be heard within four walls,—and so she put out her right hand and pushed her visitor before her into the sitting-room.

Then, keeping her back to the window, she forced Miss Wellow to turn round.

"Now tell me the truth," she commanded, "and Tiddy—above all, don't let yourself be upset, and don't get hysterical! I know what it is—you and David have had some silly quarrel. I saw from the first that you were making yourself too cheap! He can't go back to Rosaleen; he divorced her—and she's with another man. Besides, David is my brother! He wouldn't dare do such a wicked thing! You have no right, Tiddy, to accuse him of such shameful behaviour!" She spoke with quick, savage decision.

But Miss Wellow faced her with a strange, untoward courage—"I won't have you speak so of him—of David, I mean!" she exclaimed passionately, "you're his sister and ought to take his part!"

Then her voice broke, and with a touch of her old feebleness she added, "If you had heard him telling me about it, even you, Kate, who are so hard, would maybe have understood and felt sorry for him. *I* felt very sorry for him——"

"*You!*"—said Mrs. Rigby, with what appeared to the other withering contempt, "*you!*——"

"He put it very beautifully," continued Miss Wellow; her voice was now almost inaudible, but Mrs. Rigby caught the word and repeated it with terrible irony:

"Beautifully!" she said,—"beautifully!"

Matilda shrank back as though she feared the other was about to strike her, but Mrs. Rigby did not see the gesture.

"And did he tell you when he proposes to bring——" she made a scarcely perceptible pause and then shot out the words—"his bride home. If it's to-morrow, I'll make Matt take me away to-night!"

"He's not going to bring her home," said Matilda, quietly. "He's never coming back himself; they are going right away—out of England."

"A good thing too!" said Mrs. Rigby.

"He says that will be more respectful to me; he has considered my feelings, Kate—he has indeed."

"Has he? Why——" she suddenly held up a warning finger, for there was a sound of footsteps in the passage; the sound stopped outside the door, and both women instinctively held their breath, united by a common fear of servants' gossip.

There was a long pause, and then the handle of the door was slowly turned, and Mr. Rigby came into the room, his ruddy colour gone, or rather lying in curious streaks across his face, a nervous smile hovering over his lips.

He shut the door behind him and looked, with a world of interrogation and anxiety in his eyes, at his wife.

"You needn't smile," she said sharply; "this is no smiling matter!"

His eyes fell; instinctively he turned to the other, the weaker vessel. But the reproof which Mrs. Rigby had just addressed to her husband penetrated Miss Wellow's brain.

"I'm afraid I do look rather silly!" she said nervously, "wearing this dress, I mean. But, you see, knowing that now I shall never wear it, I thought I would put it on to-night."

The odd collocation of her words passed unnoticed; indeed, Mr. Rigby, even had he wished to answer her, was not given time to do so, for his wife had turned on him and was avenging in his person the heaped-up wrongs of her sex.

"It's all your fault, Matt! You were always against David going to London from the first, and you ought to have prevented his doing so! But no—you stood aside and did nothing! I suppose you guessed he might meet that—that——" her lips snapped together she would not soil them by uttering the word which to her mind alone described Rosaleen.

As her husband did not answer, suspicion grew into certainty.

"Did you know that she was there? Did you think he would see her?" she demanded.

Mr. Rigby looked mildly at his Kate. "I didn't know anything, but I did just think it possible," he said.

But his triumph, if triumph it was, was short-lived.

"Why didn't you tell me then? A decent woman would never have thought of such a thing, but men have such disgusting minds!" cried his wife sharply. She added suspiciously, "But how did you learn what's happened? Did David write to you?"

"He came into the office on his way back to the station," said Mr. Rigby, briefly. "And, Kate—I've promised to see to things for him. Rosy will join them"—he gave a little cough—"the day after to-morrow, and they will all sail for South Africa as soon as matters can be settled up. It's better so, my dear."

Suddenly Miss Wellow bent down. Her hand fumbled blindly among the soft, voluminous flounces of her skirt.

"I've got something here," she said in a muffled voice, "that I want you to give Rosy, Matt. But though I know it's there, I can't find the pocket; you know I had one put in because David once said that he didn't like a woman without a pocket in her dress. I've found it—here it is!"—she took a step forward, and standing close to her old friend, thrust into his unresisting hand a small hard substance. He looked down and saw it was the ruby ring. "You can give this to the child," she said breathlessly, "I don't want to see her again—with love from Auntie Tiddy."

But this was more than Mrs. Rigby could stand.

"Well, it's a good thing," she exclaimed to her husband, "that Tiddy takes it like that! No man would ever have dared to treat me so! But as long as she doesn't care—still, she needn't take David's part against his own sister, who has the right——"

But what right David's sister had was never explained, for Miss Wellow suddenly swayed forward; she would have fallen to the ground had not Mr. Rigby caught her.

"Why, she's fainted!" he said pitifully; "she does care—more than you think, Kate. But she will come round soon—too soon," he muttered to himself.

It was the same night, or rather the next morning, for the dawn was beginning to make its grey way into the bed-chamber of Mr. and Mrs. Rigby; it threw into dim relief the large, almost square four-poster, under the chintz-covered canopy of which the husband and wife lay, rigid as if carved in stone.

"Kate," said Matt, "are you awake?"

He could just see her head lying on the other pillow beside him. Her still abundant hair was loosened and gave her a look of youth. Tears had made a furrow down her cheeks.

"Yes," said Mrs. Rigby, "I am awake, Matt. What is it you want?"

"I'm afraid, my dear, that you are very much upset." There were understanding, sympathy, ay, and tenderness expressed in the way Mr. Rigby uttered the homely word.

His wife, for the first time in their twenty-five years of married life, felt a responsive thrill. For the first time she was unfaithful to Nat Bower.

"It's of you I'm thinking," she whispered. "I've been trying all night to forget David,—my poor little David,—but it's terrible to me to think that you, Matt, married into a family that could be guilty of such shameful behaviour!"

VI

THE DECREE MADE ABSOLUTE

James Tapster was eating his solitary, well-cooked dinner in his comfortable and handsome house, a house situated in one of the half-moon terraces which line and frame the more aristocratic side of Regent's Park, and which may indeed be said to have private grounds of their own, for each resident enjoys the use of a key to a portion of the Park entitled locally "The Enclosure."

Very early in his life Mr. Tapster had made up his mind that he would like to live in Cumberland Crescent and now he was living there; very early in his life he had decided that no one could order a plain yet palatable meal as well as he could himself, and now for some months past Mr. Tapster had given his own orders, each morning, to the cook.

To-night Mr. Tapster had already eaten his fried sole, and he was about to cut himself off a generous portion of the grilled under-cut before him, when he heard the postman's steps hurrying round the Crescent. He rose with a certain quick deliberateness, and going out into the hall, opened the front door just in time to avoid the rat-tat-tat. Then, the one letter he had expected duly in his hand, he waited till he had sat down again in front of his still empty plate before he broke the seal and glanced over the typewritten sheet of notepaper.

>   SHORTERS COURT, THROGMORTON ST.,*November 4th, 190—*.
>
>   DEAR JAMES,
>
>   In reply to your letter of yesterday's date, I have been to Bedford Row and seen Greenfield, and he thinks it probable that the decree will be made absolute to-day; in that case you will have received a wire before this letter reaches you. Your affect. Brother, WM. A. TAPSTER.

In the same handwriting as the signature were added two holograph lines: "Glad you have the children home again. Maud will be round to see them soon."

Mr. Tapster read over once again the body of the letter, and there came upon him an instinctive feeling of intense relief; then, with a not less instinctive feeling of impatience, his eyes travelled down again to the postscript—"Maud will be round to see them soon."

Well, he would see about that! But he did not exclaim, even mentally, as most men feeling as he then felt would have done, "I'll be damned if she will!" knowing the while that Maud certainly would.

His brother's letter, though most satisfactory as regarded its main point, put Mr. Tapster out of conceit with the rest of his dinner; so he rang twice and had the table cleared, frowning at the parlour-maid as she hurried through her duties, and yet not daring to rebuke her for having neglected to answer the bell the first time he rang.

After a pause, he rose and turned towards the door—but, no, he could not face the large, cheerless drawing-room upstairs; instead, he sat down by the fire, and set himself to consider his future, and, in a more hazy sense, that of his now motherless children.

But very soon, as generally happens to those who devote any time to that least profitable of occupations, Mr. Tapster found that his thoughts drifted aimlessly, not to the future where he would have them be, but to the past—that past which he desired to forget, to obliterate from his memory.

Till rather more than a year ago few men of his age—he had then been sixty, he was now sixty-one—enjoyed a pleasanter and, from his own point of view, a better-filled life than James Tapster. How he had scorned the gambler, the spendthrift, the adulterer,—in a word, all those whose actions bring about their own inevitable punishment! He had always been self-respecting and conscientious,—not a prig, mind you, but inclined rather to the serious than to the flippant side of life, and so inclining he had found contentment and great material prosperity.

Not even in those days to which he was now looking back so regretfully had Mr. Tapster always been perfectly content; but now the poor man sitting alone by his dining-room fire, only remembered what had been good and pleasant in his former state. He was aware that his brother William—and William's wife, Maud—both thought that even now he had much to be thankful for; his line of business was brisk, scarcely touched by foreign competition, his income increasing at a steady rate of progression, and his children were exceptionally healthy.

But, alas! now that, in place of a pretty little Mrs. Tapster on whom to spend easily-earned money, his substance was being squandered by a crowd of unmanageable and yet indispensable thieves,—for so Mr. Tapster voicelessly described the five servants whose loud talk and laughter were even now floating up from the basement below,—he did not feel his financial stability so comfortable a thing as he had once done.

His very children, who should now be, as he told himself complainingly, his greatest comfort, had degenerated from two sturdy, well-behaved little boys and a charming baby girl, into three unruly, fretful imps, setting him at defiance, and terrorising their two attendants, who, though carefully chosen by their Aunt Maud, did not seem to manage them as well as the old nurse who had been an ally of the ex-Mrs. Tapster.

Looking back at the whole horrible affair, for so in his own mind Mr. Tapster justly designated the divorce case in which he had figured as the successful petitioner, he wondered uneasily if he had done quite wisely—wisely, that is, for his own repute and comfort.

He knew very well that had it not been for William—or rather for Maud—he would never have found out the dreadful truth. Nay, more; he was dimly aware that but for them, and for their insistence on it as the only proper course open to him, he would never have taken action. All would have been forgiven and forgotten had not William—and more especially Maud—said he must divorce Flossy, if not for his own sake, ah! what irony! then for that of his children.

Of course he felt grateful to his brother William and to his brother's wife for all they had done for him since that sad time. Still, in the depths of his heart, Mr. Tapster felt entitled to blame, and sometimes almost to hate, his kind brother and sister. To them both—or rather to Maud—he really owed the break-up of his life, for, when all was said and done, it had to be admitted (though Maud did not like him to remind her of it) that Flossy had met the villain while staying with the William Tapsters at Boulogne. Respectable London people should have known better than to take a furnished house at a disreputable French watering-place—a place full of low English!

Sometimes it was only by a great exercise of self-control that he, James Tapster, could refrain from telling Maud what he thought of her conduct in this matter, the more so that she never seemed to understand how greatly she—and William—had been to blame.

On one occasion Maud had even said how surprised she had been that James had cared to go away to America, leaving his pretty young wife alone for as long as three months. Why hadn't she said so at the time, then? Of course, he had thought that he could leave Flossy to be looked after and kept out of mischief by Maud—and William. But he had been—in more than one sense, alas!—bitterly deceived.

Still, it's never any use crying over spilt milk, so Mr. Tapster got up from his chair and walked round the room, looking absently, as he did so, at the large Landseer engraving of which he was naturally proud. If only he could forget—put out of his mind for ever—the whole affair! Well, perhaps with the Decree being made Absolute would come oblivion.

He sat down again before the fire. Staring at the hot embers, he reminded himself that Flossy, wicked, ungrateful Flossy, had disappeared out of his life. This being so, why think of her? The very children had at last left off asking inconvenient questions about their mamma——

By the way, would Flossy still be their mamma after the Decree had been made Absolute?—so Mr. Tapster now suddenly asked himself. He hesitated perplexed.

But yes, the Decree being made Absolute would not undo, or even efface, that fact. The more so, though surely here James Tapster showed himself less logical than usual—the more so that Flossy, in spite of what Maud had always said about her, had been a loving and, in her own light-hearted way, a careful mother. But though Flossy would remain the mother of his children—odd that the Law hadn't provided for that contingency—she would soon be absolutely nothing, and less than nothing, to him, the father of those children. Mr. Tapster was a great believer in the infallibility of the Law, and he subscribed whole-heartedly to the new reading, "What Law has put asunder, let not man join together."

To-night Mr. Tapster could not help looking back with a certain complacency to his one legal adventure. Nothing could have been better done, or more admirably conducted, than the way the whole matter had been carried through. His brother William, and William's solicitor, Mr. Greenfield, had managed it all so very nicely. True, there had been a few uncomfortable moments in the witness-box, but everyone, including the Judge, had been most kind.

As for his Counsel, the leading man who makes a specialty of these sad affairs, not even James Tapster himself could have put his own case in a more delicate and moving fashion. "A gentleman possessed of considerable fortune," so had he been justly described, and Counsel, without undue insistence on irrelevant detail, had drawn a touching—and a true—picture of Mr. Tapster's one romance, his marriage eight years before to the twenty-year-old daughter of an undischarged bankrupt. Even the Petitioner had scarcely seen Flossy's dreadful ingratitude in its true colours till he had heard his Counsel's moderate comments on the case.

This evening Mr. Tapster saw Flossy's dreadful ingratitude terribly clearly, and he wondered, not for the first time, how his wife could have had the heart to break up his happy home!

Why, but for him and his offer of marriage, Flossy Ball—that had been his wife's maiden name—would have had to have earned her own living! And as she had been very pretty, very "fetching," she would probably have married some good-for-nothing young fellow of her own age lacking the means to support a wife in decent comfort,—such a fellow, for instance, as the wretched "Co." in the case. While with Mr. Tapster—why, she had had everything the heart of woman could wish for, a good home, beautiful clothes, and the being waited on hand and foot. A strange choking feeling came into his throat as he thought of how good he had been to Flossy, and how very bad had been her return for that kindness.

But this—this was dreadful! He was actually thinking of her again, and not, as he had meant to do, of himself and his poor, motherless children. Time enough to think of Flossy when he had news of her again. If her lover did not marry her—and from what Mr. Greenfield had discovered about him, it was most improbable that he would ever be in a position to do so—she would certainly reappear on the Tapster horizon; Mr. Greenfield said "they" always did. In that case, it was arranged that William should pay her a weekly allowance. Mr. Tapster, always, as he now reminded himself sadly, ready to do the generous thing, had fixed that allowance at three pounds a week—a sum which had astonished, in fact quite staggered, Mr. Greenfield's head clerk, a very decent fellow, by the way.

"Of course, it shall be as you wish, Mr. Tapster, but you should think of the future and of your children. A hundred and fifty pounds a year is a large sum; you may feel it a tax, sir, as years go on———"

"That is enough," Mr. Tapster had answered, kindly but firmly; "you have done your duty in laying that side of the case before me. I have, however, decided on the amount named; should I see reason to alter my mind, our arrangement leaves it open to me at any time to lower the allowance."

But though this conversation had taken place some months ago, and though Mr. Tapster still held true to his generous resolve, as yet Flossy had not reappeared.

Mr. Tapster sometimes told himself that if he only knew where she was, what she was doing,—whether she was still with that young fellow, for instance,—he would think much less about her than he did now. Only last night, when going for a moment into the night nursery,—poor Mr. Tapster now only enjoyed his children's company when he was quite sure that they were asleep,—he had had an extraordinary, almost a physical, impression of Flossy's presence; he certainly had felt a faint whiff of her favourite perfume. Flossy had been fond of scent, and though Maud always said that the use of scent was most unladylike, he, James, did not dislike it.

With sudden soreness Mr. Tapster now recalled the one letter Flossy had written to him just before the actual hearing of the divorce suit.

It had been a wild, oddly-worded appeal to him to take her back, not—as Maud had at once perceived on reading the letter—because she was sorry for the terrible thing she had done, but simply because she was beginning to hanker after her children. Maud had described the letter as shameless and unwomanly in the extreme; and even William, who had never judged his pretty young sister-in-law as severely as his wife had always done, had observed sadly that Flossy seemed quite unaware of the magnitude of her offence against God and man.

Mr. Tapster, who prided himself on his sharp ears, suddenly heard a curious little sound—he knew it for that of the front door being first opened and then shut again, extremely quietly. He half rose from his chair by the fire, then sat down again, heavily.

By Maud's advice he always locked the area gate himself, when he came home each evening. But how foolish of Maud—such a sensible woman too,—to think that servants and their evil ways could be circumvented so easily! Of course, the maids went in and out by the front door in the evening, and the policeman—a most respectable officer standing at point duty a few yards lower down the road—must be well aware of these disgraceful "goings on."

For the first two or three months of his widowerhood (how else could he term his present peculiar wifeless condition?) there had been a constant coming and going of servants, first chosen, and then dismissed, by Maud. At last she had suggested that her brother-in-law should engage a lady housekeeper, and the luckless James Tapster had even interviewed several applicants for the post after they had been chosen—sifted out, as it were—by Maud. Unfortunately they had all been each more or less of his own age; and plain—very plain; while he, naturally enough, would have preferred to see something young and pretty about him again.

It was over this housekeeper question that he had at last escaped from Maud's domestic thraldom, for his sister-in-law, offended by his rejection of each of her candidates, had declared that she would take no more trouble about his household affairs! Nay, more; she had reminded him with a smile which she had honestly tried to make pleasant, that there is, after all, no fool like an old fool—about women! This insinuation had made Mr. Tapster very angry, and straightway he had engaged a respectable cook-housekeeper, and, although he had soon become aware that the woman was feathering her own nest,—James Tapster, as you will have divined ere now, was fond of good workaday phrases,—yet she had a pleasant, respectful manner, and kept rough order among the younger servants.

Mr. Tapster's sister-in-law only now interfered where his children were concerned. Never having been herself a mother, she had, of course, been able to form a clear and unprejudiced judgment as to how children, and especially as to how little boys, should be physically and mentally trained.

As yet, however, Maud had not been very successful with her two nephews and infant niece, but this was doubtless owing to the fact that there had been something gravely amiss with each of the five nurses who had been successively engaged by her during the last year.

The elder of Mr. Tapster's sons was six and the second four; the youngest child, a little girl named unfortunately Flora after her mother, was three years old. There had been a fourth, Flossy's second baby, also a girl, who had only lived one day. All this being so, was it not strange that a young matron who had led, for some four years out of the eight years her married life had lasted, so wholly womanly and domestic an existence as had fallen to the lot of Flossy, should have been led astray by the meretricious allurements of unlawful love?—Maud's striking thought and phrase this.

And yet Flossy, in spite of her frivolity, had somehow managed the children far better than Maud was now able to do. At the present time, so Mr. Tapster admitted to himself with something very like an inward groan, his two sons possessed every vice of which masculine infancy is capable. They had become—so he was told by their indignant nurses—the terror of the well-behaved children who shared with them the pleasures of the Park Enclosure, where they took their daily exercise; and Baby, once so sweet and good, was now very fretful and peevish.

Again the train of Mr. Tapster's mournful thoughts was disturbed by a curious little sound—that of someone creeping softly down the staircase leading from the upper floors.

Once more he half rose from his chair, only to fall heavily back again with a look of impotent annoyance on his round, whiskered face. Where was the use of his going out into the hall and catching Nurse on her way to the kitchen? Maud had declared, very early in the day, that there should be as little communication as possible between the kitchen and the nursery; but Mr. Tapster sometimes found himself in secret sympathy with the two women whose disagreeable duty it was to be always with his three turbulent children.

Mr. Tapster frowned and stared gloomily into the fire; then he suddenly pulled himself together rather sharply, for the door behind him had slowly swung open. This was intolerable! The parlour-maid had again and again been told that, whatever might have been the case in her former places, no door in Mr. Tapster's house was to be opened without the preliminary of a respectful knock.

Fortified by the memory of what had been a positive order, he turned round and nerved himself to deliver the necessary rebuke; but instead of the shifty-eyed, impudent-looking woman he had thought to see, there stood close to him, so close that he could almost have touched her— Flossy, his wife, or rather the woman who, though no longer his wife, had still, as he had been informed to his discomfiture, the right to bear his name.

A very strange feeling, and one so complicated that it sat uneasily upon him, took instant possession of Mr. Tapster—anger, surprise, and relief warred with one another in his heart.

Then he began to think that his eyes must be playing him some curious trick, for the figure at which he was staring remained strangely still and motionless.

Was it possible that his mind, dwelling constantly on Flossy, had evoked her wraith? But, no; looking up in startled silence at the still figure standing before him, he realised that not so would memory have conjured up the pretty, bright little woman of whom he had once been proud. Flossy still looked pretty, but she was thin and pale, and there were dark rings round her eyes; also her dress was worn, her hat curiously shabby.

As Mr. Tapster stared up at her, noting these things, one of her hands began playing nervously with the fringe of the dining-table cover, and the other sought the back of what had once been one of her dining-room chairs.

As he watched her making these slight movements, nature so far reasserted itself that a feeling of poignant regret, of pity for her—as well as, of course, a much larger share of pity for himself—came over James Tapster.

Had Flossy spoken then,—had she possessed the intuitive knowledge of men which is the gift of so many otherwise unintelligent women,—the whole of Mr. Tapster's future, to say nothing of her own, might have been different, and, it may be suggested, happier.

But the moment of softening and mansuetude slipped quickly by, and was succeeded by a burst of anger, for Mr. Tapster suddenly became aware that Flossy's left hand, the little thin hand resting on the back of the chair, was holding two keys which he recognised at once as his property. The one was a replica of the latch-key which always hung on his watch-chain, while the other and larger key, to which was attached a brass tab bearing the name of

Tapster and the address of the house, gave access to the Enclosure Garden opposite Cumberland Crescent.

Avoiding her eager, pitiful look, Mr. Tapster set himself to realise, with a shrewdness for which William and Maud would never have given him credit, what Flossy's possession of those two keys had meant during the last few months.

This woman, who both was and was not Mrs. Tapster, had retained the power to come freely in and out of *his* house! She had been able to make her way, with or without the connivance of the servants, into *his* children's nursery at any hour of the day or night convenient to herself. With the aid of that Enclosure key she had no doubt often seen the children during their daily walk! In a word, Flossy had been able to enjoy all the privileges of motherhood while having forfeited all those of happy wifehood!

His mind hastened heavily on—what a fool he must have looked before his servants, how they must have laughed to think that he was being so deceived and taken in! Why, even the policeman who stood at point duty outside must have known all about it!

Small wonder that Mr. Tapster felt extremely incensed; small wonder that his heart, hardening, solidifying, expelled any feeling of pity provoked by Flossy's sad and downcast appearance.

"I must request you," he said, in a voice which even to himself sounded harsh and needlessly loud, "to give up those keys which you hold in your hand. You have no right to their possession, and I grieve to think that you took advantage of my great distress of mind not to return them with the things of which I sent you a list by my brother William. I cannot believe"—and now Mr. Tapster lied as only the very truthful can lie on occasion—"I cannot believe, I say, that you have taken advantage of my having overlooked them, and that you have ever before to-night forced yourself into this house! Still less can I believe that you have taught our—*my*—children to deceive their father!"

Even when uttering his first sentence he had noticed that there had come over Flossy's face—which was thinner, if quite as pretty and youthful-looking as when he had last seen it—an expression of obstinacy which he had once well known and always dreaded. It had been Flossy's one poor weapon against her husband's superior sense and power of getting his own way, and sometimes it had vanquished him in that fair fight which is always being waged between the average husband and wife.

"You are right," she cried passionately; "I have not taught the children to deceive you! I have never come into this house until I felt sure that they were asleep and alone, though I've often wondered that they never woke up and knew that their own mother was there! But more than once, James, I've felt like going after that Society which looks after badly-treated children—for the last nurse you had for them was so cruel! If she hadn't left you soon I should have *had* to do something. I used to feel desperate when I saw her shake Baby in her pram; why, one day, in the Enclosure, a lady spoke to her about it, and threatened to tell her—her mistress——"

Flossy's voice sank to a shamed whisper. The tears were rolling down her cheeks; she was speaking in angry gasps, and what she said actually made James Tapster feel, what he knew full well he had no reason to feel, ashamed of himself.

"That is why"—she went on—"that is why I have, as you say, forced myself into your house, and why, too, I have now come here to ask you to forgive me—to take me back—just for the sake of the children."

Mr. Tapster's mind was one that travelled surely if slowly. He saw his chance and seized it.

"And why," he said impressively, "had that woman—the nurse, I mean—no mistress? Tell me that, Flossy. You should have thought of all that before you behaved as you did!"

"I didn't know—I didn't think——"

Mr. Tapster finished the sentence for her. "You didn't think," he observed impressively, "that I should ever find you out."

Then there came over him a morbid wish to discover—to learn from her own lips—why Flossy had done such a shameful and extraordinary thing as to be unfaithful to her marriage vow.

"Whatever made you behave so?" he asked in a low voice. "I wasn't unkind to you, was I? You had a nice, comfortable home, hadn't you?"

"I was mad," she answered with a touch of sharp weariness. "I don't suppose I could ever make you understand, and yet"—she looked at him deprecatingly—"I suppose, James, that you too were young once, and—and—mad?"

Mr. Tapster stared at Flossy. What extraordinary things she said! Of course he had been young once; for the matter of that he didn't feel old—not to say old—even now. But he had always been perfectly sane—she knew that well enough! As for her calling herself mad, that was a mere figure of speech. Of course, in a sense she had been mad to do what she had done, and he was glad that she now understood this, but her saying so simply begged the whole question, and left him no wiser than he was before.

There was a long, tense silence between them. Then Mr. Tapster slowly rose from his armchair and faced his wife.

"I see," he said, "that William was right. I mean, I suppose I may take it that that young fellow has gone and left you?"

"Yes," she said, with a curious indifference, "he has gone and left me. His father made him take a job out in Brazil just after the case was through."

"And what have you been doing since then?" asked Mr. Tapster suspiciously. "How have you been living?"

"His father gives me a pound a week." Flossy still spoke with that curious indifference. "I tried to get something to do"—she hesitated, then offered the lame explanation, "just to have something to do, for I've been awfully lonely and miserable, James. But I don't seem to be able to get anything."

"If you had written to Mr. Greenfield or to William, they would have told you that I had arranged for you to have an allowance," he said, and then again he fell into silence....

Mr. Tapster was seeing a vision of himself magnanimous, forgiving,—taking the peccant Flossy back to his heart, and becoming once more, in a material sense, comfortable! If he acceded to her wish, if he made up his mind to forgive her, he would have to begin life all over again, move away from Cumberland Crescent to some distant place where the story was not known,—perhaps to Clapham, where he had spent his boyhood.

But how about Maud? How about William? How about the very considerable expense to which he had been put in connection with the divorce proceedings? Was all that money to be wasted?

Mr. Tapster suddenly saw the whole of his little world rising up in judgment, smiling pityingly at his folly and weakness. During the whole of a long and of what had been, till this last year, a very prosperous life, Mr. Tapster had always steered his safe course by what may be called the compass of public opinion, and now, when navigating an unknown sea, he could not afford to throw that compass overboard, so——

"No," he said. "No, Flossy. It would not be right for me to take you back. *It wouldn't do.*"

"Wouldn't it?" she asked piteously. "Oh! James, don't say no like that, all at once! People do forgive each other—sometimes. I don't ask you to be as kind to me as you were before; only to let me come home and see after the children!"

But Mr. Tapster shook his head. The children! Always the children! He noticed, even now, that she didn't say a word of wanting to come back to *him*; and yet he had been such a kind, nay, if Maud were to be believed, such a foolishly indulgent, husband.

And then Flossy looked so different. Mr. Tapster felt as if a stranger were standing there before him. Her appearance of poverty shocked him. Had she looked well and prosperous, he would have felt injured, and yet her pinched face and shabby clothes certainly repelled him. So again he shook his head, and there came into his face a look which Flossy had always known in the old days to spell finality; when he again spoke she saw that her knowledge had not misled her.

"I don't want to be unkind," he said ponderously. "If you will only go to William, or write to him if you would rather not go to the office,"—Mr. Tapster did not like to think that anyone once closely connected with him should "look like that" in his brother's office,—"he will tell you what you had better do. I'm quite ready to make you a handsome allowance—in fact, it's all arranged. You need not have anything more to do with that fellow's father—an Army Colonel, isn't he?—and his pound a week; but William thinks, and I must say I agree, that you ought to go back to your maiden name, Flossy, as being more fair to me."

"And am I never to see the children again?" she asked.

"No; it wouldn't be right for me to let you do so."

He hesitated, then added, "They don't miss you any more now,"—with no unkindly intent he concluded, "soon they'll have forgotten you altogether."

And then, just as Mr. Tapster was hesitating, seeking for a suitable and not unkindly sentence of farewell, he saw a very strange, almost a desperate, look come over Flossy's face, and, to his surprise, she suddenly turned and left the room, closing the door very carefully behind her.

He stared after her. How very odd of her to say nothing! And what a queer look had come over her face! He could not help feeling hurt that she had not thanked him for what he knew to be a very generous and unusual provision on the part of an injured husband.... Mr. Tapster took a silk handkerchief out of his pocket and passed it twice over his face, then once more he sought and sank into the armchair by the fire.

Even now he still felt keenly conscious of Flossy's nearness. What could she be doing? Then he straightened himself and listened.

Yes, it was as he feared; she had gone upstairs—upstairs to look at the children, for now he could hear her coming down again. How obstinate she was—how obstinate and ungrateful! Mr. Tapster wished he had the courage to go out into the hall and face her in order to tell her how wrong her conduct was. Why, she had actually kept the keys—those keys that were his property!

Suddenly he heard her light footsteps hurrying down the hall; now she was opening the front door,—it slammed, and again Mr. Tapster felt pained to think how strangely indifferent Flossy was to his interests. Why, what would the servants think, hearing the front door slam like that?

But still, now that it was over, he was glad the interview had taken place, for henceforth—or so at least Mr. Tapster believed—the Flossy of the past, the bright, pretty, prosperous Flossy of whom he had been so proud, would cease to haunt him.

He remembered with a feeling of relief that she was going to his brother William; of course she would then, among greater renunciations, be compelled to return the two keys, for they—that is, his brother and himself—would have her in their power. They would not behave unkindly to her—far from it; in fact, they would arrange for her to live with some quiet, religious lady in a country town a few hours from London. Mr. Tapster had not evolved this scheme for himself; it had been done in a similar case—one of those cases which, in the long ago, when he was still a single man, had aroused his pitying contempt for husbands who allow themselves to be deceived.

Then Mr. Tapster began going over each incident of the strange little interview, for he wanted to tell his brother William exactly what had taken place.

His conscience was quite clear except with regard to one matter, and that, after all, needn't be mentioned to William. He felt rather ashamed of having asked the question which had provoked so wild an answer—so unexpected a retort.

Mad? What had Flossy meant by asking him if he had ever been mad? No one had ever used the word in connection with James Tapster before—save once. Oddly enough, that occasion also had been connected with Flossy in a way; for it had happened when he had gone to tell William and Maud of his engagement.

It was on a fine day nine years ago come this May, and he had found William and William's wife walking in their garden on Haverstock Hill. His kind brother, as always, had been most sympathetic, and had even made a suitable joke—Mr. Tapster remembered it very sadly to-night—concerning the spring and a young man's fancy; but Maud had been really disagreeable. She had said, "It's no use talking to you, James, for you're mad—quite mad!" He had argued the matter out with her good-temperedly, and William had supported him in pointing out that he was doing an eminently sane thing in marrying Flossy Ball. But Maud again and again had exclaimed, in her determined, aggravating voice, "I say you are mad. They don't let lunatics marry—and just now you *are* a lunatic, James!"

Strange that he should remember all this to-night; for, after all, it had nothing to do with the present state of affairs.

Mr. Tapster felt rather shaken and nervous; he pulled out his repeater watch; but, alas! it was still very early—only ten minutes to nine. He couldn't go to bed yet. Perhaps he would do well to join a club. He had always thought rather poorly of men who belonged to clubs,—most of them were idle, lazy fellows; but still, circumstances alter cases.

Suddenly he began to wish that Flossy had remained a little longer.

He thought of all sorts of things—improving, kindly remarks—he would have liked to say to her. He blamed himself for not having offered her any refreshment; she would probably have refused to take anything, but still, it was wrong on his part not to have thought of it. A pound a week for everything! No wonder she looked half starved. Why, his own household bills, exclusive of wine or beer, had worked out, since he had had this new expensive housekeeper, at something like fifteen shillings a head—a fact which he had managed to conceal from Maud, who "did" her William so well on exactly ten shillings and nine-pence all round!

It struck nine from the neighbouring church where Mr. Tapster had sittings,—but where he seldom was able to go on Sunday mornings, for he was proud of being among those old-fashioned folk who still regard Sunday as essentially a day of rest,—and there came a sudden sound of hoarse shouting from the road outside.

Though he was glad of anything that broke the oppressive silence with which he felt encompassed, Mr. Tapster found time to tell himself that it was disgraceful that vulgar street brawlers should invade so quiet a residential thoroughfare as Cumberland Crescent. But order would soon be restored, for the sound of a policeman's whistle cut sharply through the air.

The noise, however, continued. He could hear the tramp of feet hurrying past his house, and then leaving the pavement for the other side of the road. What could be the matter? Something very exciting must be going on just opposite his front door—that is, close to the Enclosure railings.

Mr. Tapster got up from his chair, and walked in a leisurely way to the wide window; he drew aside the thick red rep curtains, and lifted a corner of the blind.

Then, through the slightly foggy haze, he saw that which greatly surprised him and made him feel actively indignant, for a string of people, men, women, and boys, were hurrying into the Enclosure garden—that sacred place set apart for the exclusive use of the nobility and gentry who lived in Cumberland Crescent and the adjoining terraces.

What an abominable thing! Why, the grass would be all trampled down; and these dirty people, these slum folk who seem to spring out of the earth when anything of a disagreeable or shameful nature is taking place—a fire, for instance, or a brawl—might easily bring infectious diseases on to those gravel paths where the little Tapsters and their like run about playing their innocent games. Some careless person had evidently left the gate unlocked, and the fight, or whatever it was, must be taking place inside the Enclosure!

Had this been an ordinary night, Mr. Tapster would have gone back to the fire, but now the need for human companionship was so strong upon him that he stayed at the window, and went on staring at the curious shadow-filled scene.

Soon he saw with satisfaction that something like order was to be restored. A stalwart policeman—in fact, his friend the officer who was always at point duty some yards from his house—now stood at the gate of the Enclosure, forbidding any further passing through.

Mr. Tapster tried in vain to see what was going on inside the railings, but everything beyond the brightly-lighted road was wrapped in grey darkness. Someone suddenly held up high a flaming torch, and the watcher at the window saw that the shadowy crowd which had managed to force its way into the Park hung together, like bees swarming, on the further lawn through which flowed the ornamental water. With the gleaming of the yellow, wavering light there had fallen a sudden hush and silence, and Mr. Tapster wondered uneasily what those people were doing there, and what it was they were pressing forward so eagerly to see.

Then he realised that it must have been a fight after all, for now the crowd was parting in two, and down the lane so formed Mr. Tapster saw coming towards the gate, and so in a sense towards himself, a rather pitiful little procession. Someone had evidently been injured, and that seriously, for four men, bearing a sheep-hurdle on which lay a huddled mass, were walking slowly towards the guarded gate, and he heard distinctly the gruffly uttered words: "Stand back, please—stand back there! We're going to cross the road."

The now large crowd suddenly swayed forward; indeed, to Mr. Tapster's astonished eyes, they seemed to be actually making a rush for his house; and a moment later they were pressing round his area railings.

Looking down on the upturned faces below him, Mr. Tapster was very glad that a stout pane of glass stood between himself and the sinister-looking men and women who seemed to be staring up at him, or rather at his windows, with faces full of cruel, wolfish curiosity.

He let the blind fall to gently. His interest in the vulgar, sordid scene had suddenly died down; the drama was now over; in a moment the crowd would disperse, the human vermin—but Mr. Tapster would never have used, even to himself, so coarse an expression—would be on their way back to their burrows. But before he had even time to rearrange the curtains in their right folds, there came a sudden, loud, persistent knocking at his front door.

Mr. Tapster turned sharply round, feeling justly incensed. Of course he knew what it was,—some good-for-nothing urchin finding a vent for his excited feelings. While it was quite proper that the police should have hurried on with their still burden to the nearest hospital or workhouse infirmary, they should have left at least one constable to keep order. His parlour-maid, who was never in any hurry to open the door—she had once kept him waiting ten minutes when he had forgotten his latch-key—would certainly take no notice of this unseemly noise, but he, James Tapster, would himself hurry out and try and catch the delinquent, take his name and address, and thoroughly frighten him.

As he reached the door of the dining-room Mr. Tapster heard the front door open—open, too, and this was certainly very surprising, from the outside! In the hall he saw that it was a policeman—in fact, the officer on point duty close by—who had opened his front door, and apparently with a latch-key.

In the moment that elapsed before the constable spoke, Mr. Tapster's mind had had time to formulate a new theory. How strange he had never heard that the police have means of access to every house on their beat! The fact surprised but did not alarm him, for our hero was one of the great army of law-abiding citizens in whose eyes a policeman is no human being, subject to the same laws, the same temptations and passions which afflict ordinary humanity. No, no; in Mr. Tapster's eyes a constable could do no wrong, although he might occasionally stretch a point to oblige such a man as was Mr. Tapster himself.

But what was the constable saying—speaking, as constables always do to the Mr. Tapsters of this world, in respectful and subdued tones?

"Can I just come in and speak to you, sir? There's been a sad accident—your lady fallen in the water; we found these keys in her pocket, and then someone said she was Mrs. Tapster,"—and the policeman held out the two keys which had played a not unimportant part in Mr. Tapster's interview with Flossy.

"A man on the bridge saw her go in," went on the policeman, "so she wasn't in the water long—something like a quarter of an hour—for we soon found her. I suppose you would like her taken upstairs, sir?"

"No, no," stammered Mr. Tapster, "not upstairs. The children are upstairs."

Mr. Tapster's round, prominent eyes were shadowed with a great horror and an even greater surprise. He stood staring at the man before him, his hands clasped in a wholly unconscious gesture of supplication.

The constable gradually edged himself backwards into the dining-room. Realising that he must take on himself the onus of decision, he gave a quiet look round.

"If that's the case," he said firmly, "we had better bring her in here. That sofa that you have there, sir, will do nicely, for her to be laid upon while they try to bring her round. We've got a doctor already——"

Mr. Tapster bent his head; he was too much bewildered to propose any other plan; and then he turned—turned to see his hall invaded by a strange and sinister quartette. It was composed of two policemen and of two of those loafers of whom he so greatly disapproved; they were carrying a hurdle, from which Mr. Tapster quickly averted his eyes.

But though he was able to shut out the sight he feared to see, he could not prevent himself from hearing certain sounds—those, for instance, made by the two loafers, who breathed with ostentatious difficulty as if to show they were unaccustomed to bearing even so comparatively light a burden as Flossy drowned.

There came a sudden short whisper-filled delay; the doorway of the dining-room was found to be too narrow, and the hurdle was perforce left in the hall.

An urgent voice, full of wholly unconscious irony, muttered in Mr. Tapster's ear: "Of course you would like to see her, sir," and he felt himself being propelled forward. Making an effort to bear himself so that he should not feel afterwards ashamed of his lack of nerve, he forced himself to stare with dread-filled yet fascinated eyes at that which had just been laid upon the leather sofa.

Flossy's hat—the shabby hat which had shocked Mr. Tapster's sense of what was seemly—had gone; her fair hair had all come down, and hung in pale, gold wisps about the face already fixed in the soft dignity which seems so soon to drape the features of those who die by drowning. Her widely-opened eyes were now wholly emptied of the anguish with which they had gazed on Mr. Tapster in this very room less than an hour ago. Her mean brown serge gown, from which the water was still dripping, clung closely to her limbs, revealing the slender body which had four times endured, on behalf of Mr. Tapster, the greatest of woman's natural ordeals. But that thought, it is scarcely necessary to say, did not come to add an extra pang to those which that unfortunate man was now suffering; for Mr. Tapster naturally thought maternity was in every married woman's day's work—and pleasure.

It might have been a moment, for all that he knew, or it might have been an hour, when at last something came to relieve the unbearable tension of Mr. Tapster's feelings. He had been standing aside helpless, aware of and yet not watching the efforts made to restore Flossy to consciousness.

The doctor raised himself and straightened his cramped shoulders and tired arms. With a look of great concern on his face he approached the bereaved husband.

"I'm afraid it's no good," he said; "the shock of the plunge in the cold water probably killed her. She was evidently in poor health, and—and ill-nourished. But, of course, we shall go on for some time longer, and——"

But whatever he had meant to say remained unspoken, for a telegraph boy, with the impudence natural to his kind, was forcing his way into and through the crowded room.

"James Tapster, Esquire?" he cried in a high, childish treble.

The master of the house held out his hand mechanically. He took the buff envelope and stared down at it, sufficiently master of himself to perceive that some fool had apparently imagined Cumberland Crescent to be in South London; before his eyes swam the line, "Delayed in transmission." Then, opening the envelope, he saw the message for which he had now been waiting so eagerly for some days, but it was with indifference that he read the words:

"*The Decree has been made Absolute.*"